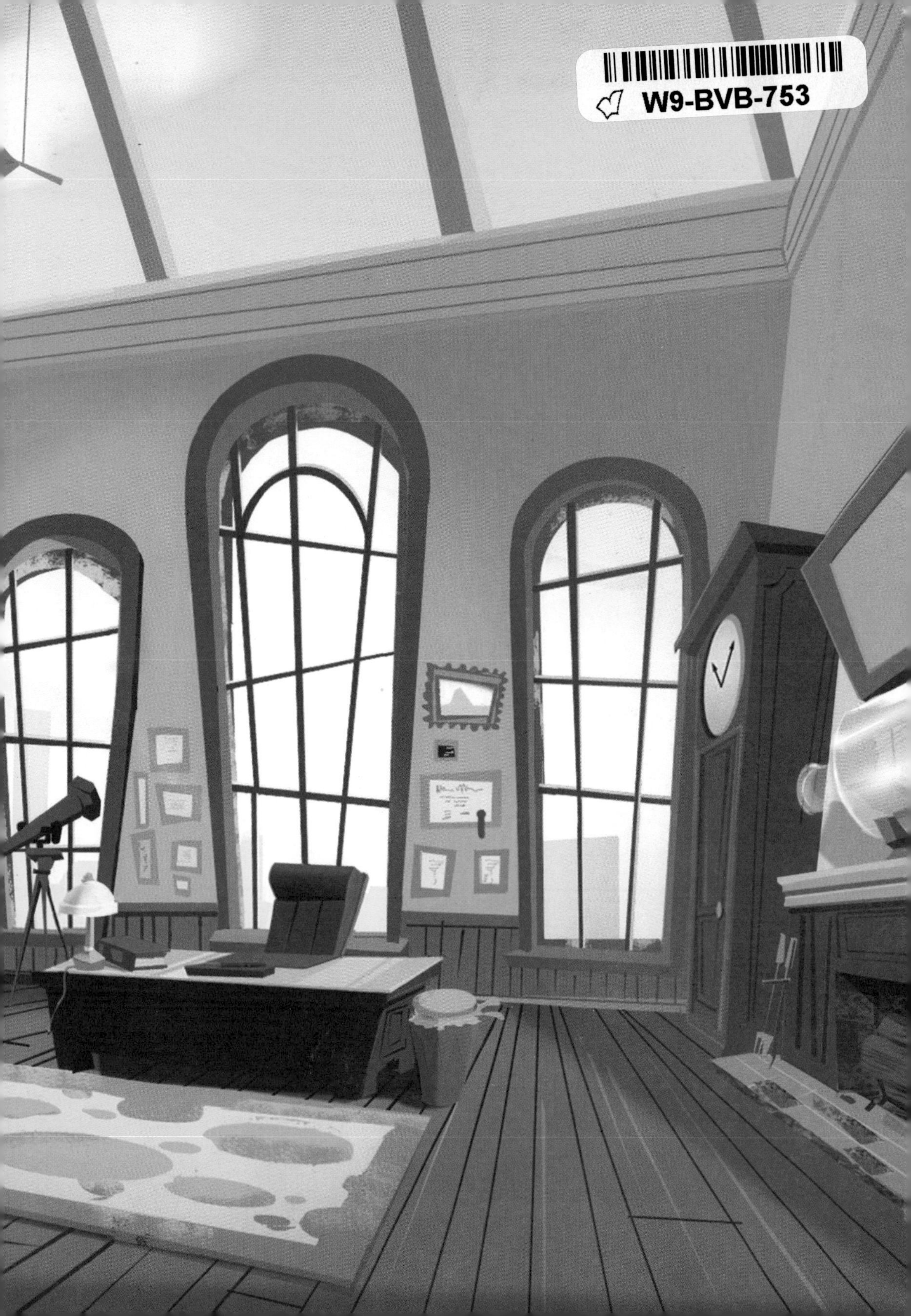

BARRY THE MOUSTACHE

Text by Geronimo Stilton
Cover by ALESSANDRO MUSCILLO (artist) and CHRISTIAN ALIPRANDI (colorist)
Editorial supervision by ALESSANDRA BERELLO (Atlantyca S.p.A.)
Editing by LISA CAPIOTTO (Atlantyca S.p.A.)
Script by DARIO SICCHIO
Art by ALESSANDRO MUSCILLO
Color by CHRISTIAN ALIPRANDI
Original Lettering by MARIA LETIZIA MIRABELLA

Special thanks to ANITA DENTI

Based on an original idea by ELISABETTA DAMI.
Based on episode 5 of the Geronimo Stilton animated series "Barry il Baffetto" ["*Barry the Moustache*"] written by TEMPLE
MATHEWS storyboard by PIER DI GIÀ and LISA ARIOL!
Preview based on episode 6 of the Geronimo Stilton animated series "Giù le zampe, faccia di fontina!" ["*Paws Off, Cheddarface!*"]
written by CATHERINE CUENCA & PATRICK REGNARD storyboard by PIER DI GIÀ and PATRIZIA NASI

www.geronimostilton.com

JAYJAY JACKSON — Production
WILSON RAMOS JR. — Lettering
JEFF WHITMAN — Managing Editor
JIM SALICRUP
Editor-in-Chief

ISBN: 978-1-5458-0477-3

Printed in India
June 2020

Papercutz books may be purchased for business or promotional use.
For information on bulk purchases please contact
Macmillan Corporate and Premium Sales
Department at (800) 221-7945x5442.

Distributed by Macmillan
First Printing

Geronimo Stilton™ Reporter

#5 BARRY THE MOUSTACHE
By Geronimo Stilton

PAPERCUTZ™
NEW YORK

Geronimo Stilton ™
Reporter

PAPERCUTZ ™

Geronimo Stilton GRAPHIC NOVELS AVAILABLE FROM PAPERCUTZ

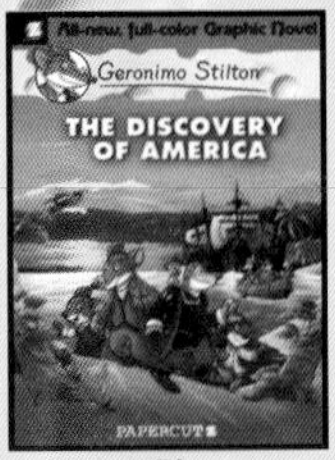
#1
"The Discovery of America"

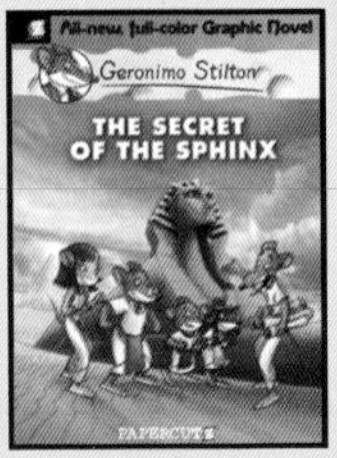
#2
"The Secret of the Sphinx"

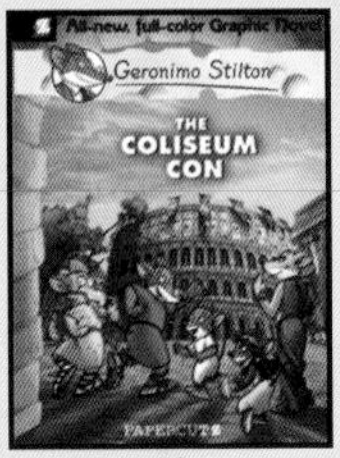
#3
"The Coliseum Con"

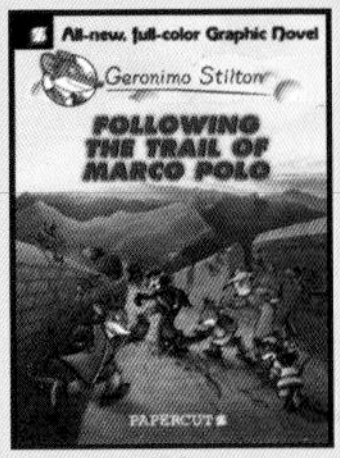
#4
"Following the Trail of Marco Polo"

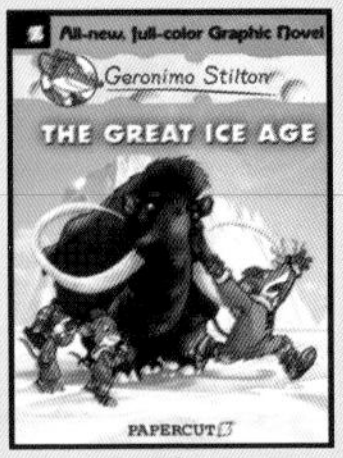
#5
"The Great Ice Age"

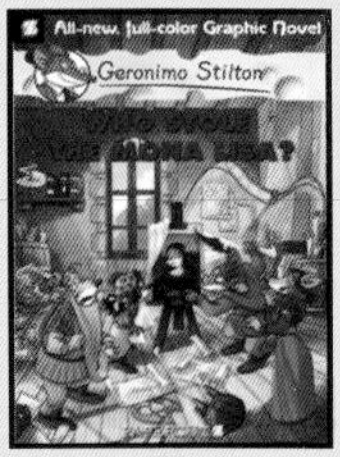
#6
"Who Stole The Mona Lisa?"

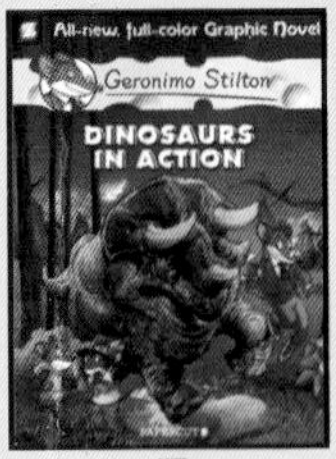
#7
"Dinosaurs in Action"

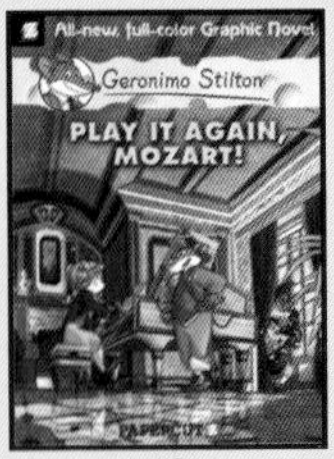
#8
"Play It Again, Mozart!"

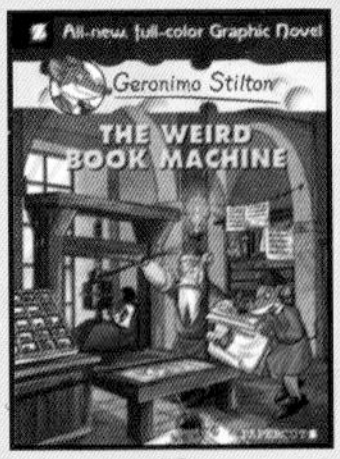
#9
"The Weird Book Machine"

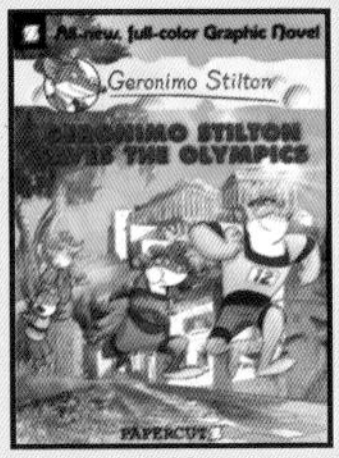
#10
"Geronimo Stilton Saves the Olympics"

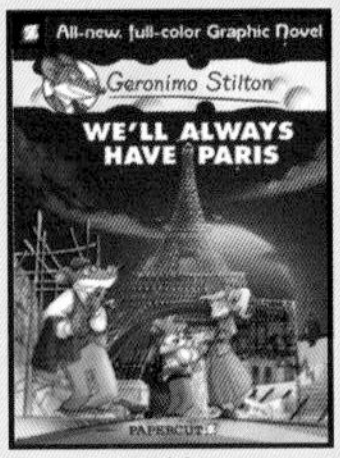
#11
"We'll Always Have Paris"

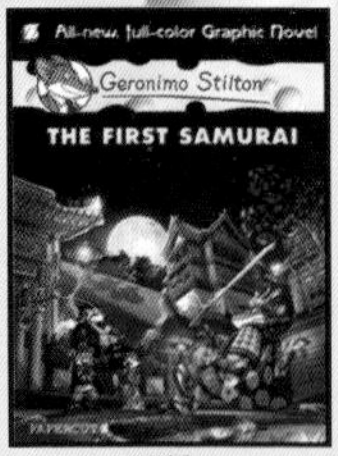
#12
"The First Samurai"

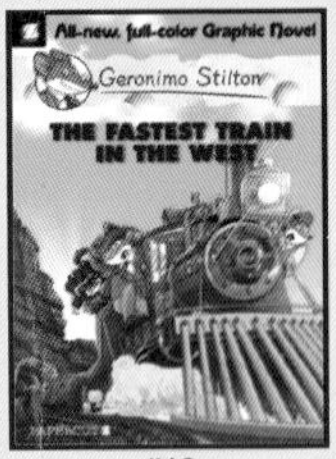
#13
"The Fastest Train in the West"

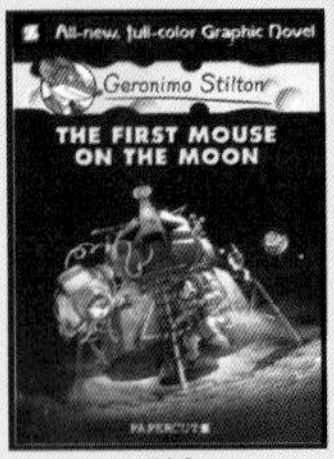
#14
"The First Mouse on the Moon"

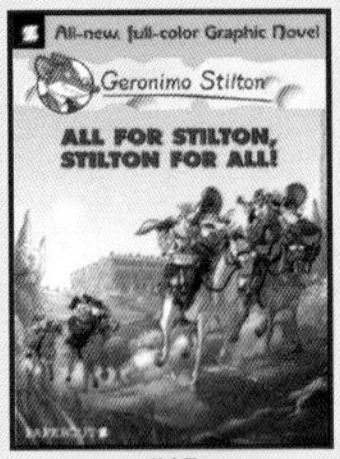
#15
"All for Stilton, Stilton for All!"

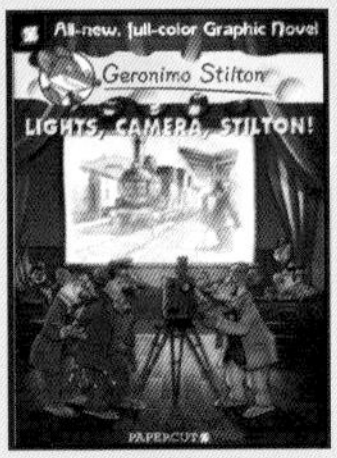
#16
"Lights, Camera, Stilton!"

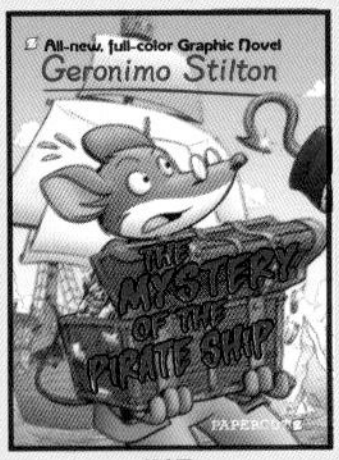
#17
"The Mystery of the Pirate Ship"

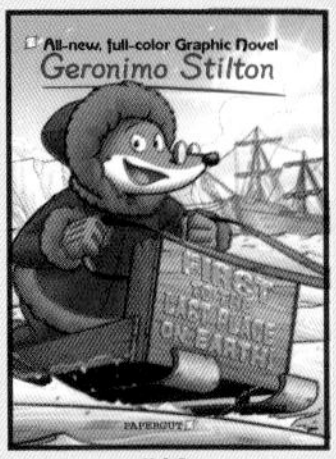
#18
"First to the Last Place on Earth"

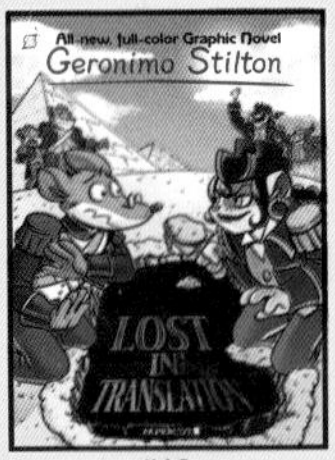
#19
"Lost in Translation"

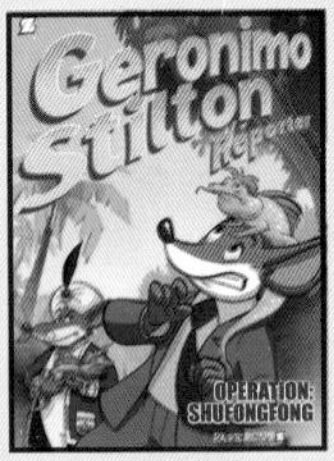
GERONIMO STILTON REPORTER #1
"Operation ShuFongfong"

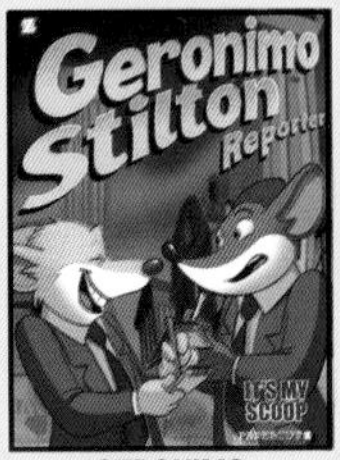
GERONIMO STILTON REPORTER #2
"It's My Scoop"

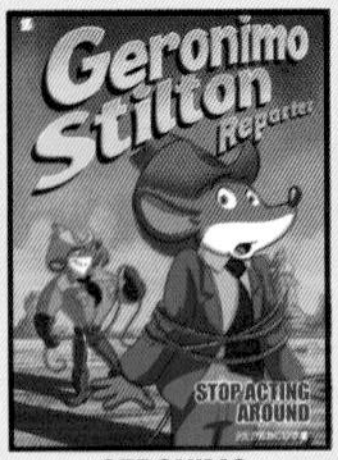
GERONIMO STILTON REPORTER #3
"Stop Acting Around"

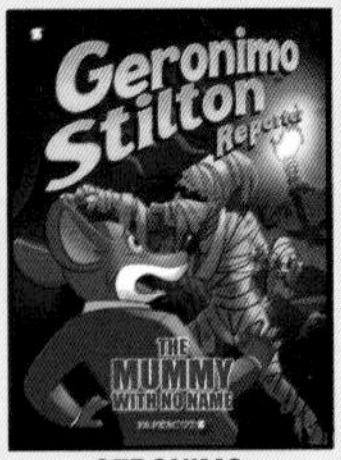
GERONIMO STILTON REPORTER #4
"The Mummy with No Name"

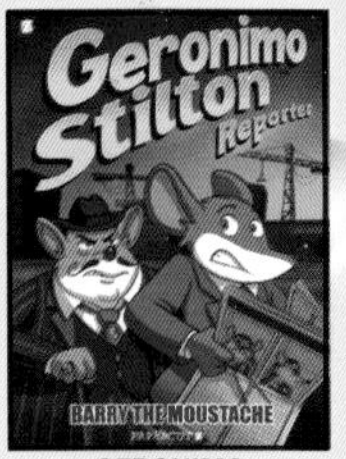
GERONIMO STILTON REPORTER #5
"Barry the Moustache"

...ALSO AVAILABLE WHEREVER E-BOOKS ARE SOLD!

See more at papercutz.com

COMING SOON

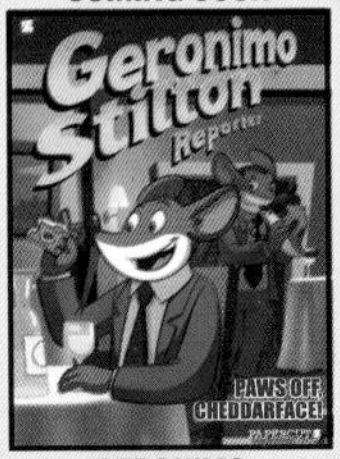
GERONIMO STILTON REPORTER #6
"Paws Off, Cheddarface!"

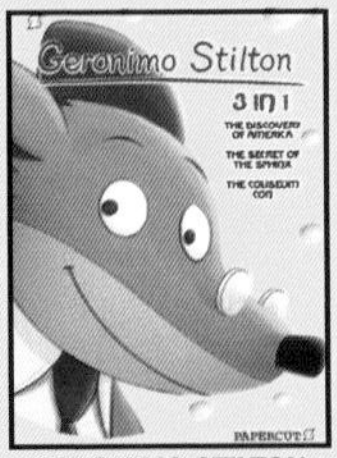
GERONIMO STILTON 3 in 1 #1

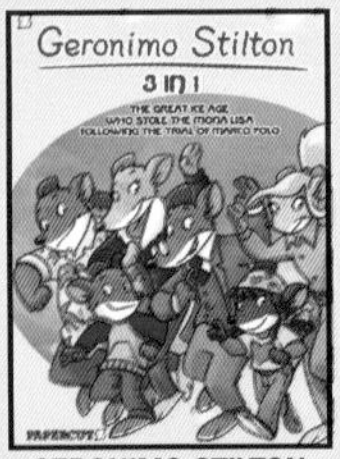
GERONIMO STILTON 3 in 1 #2

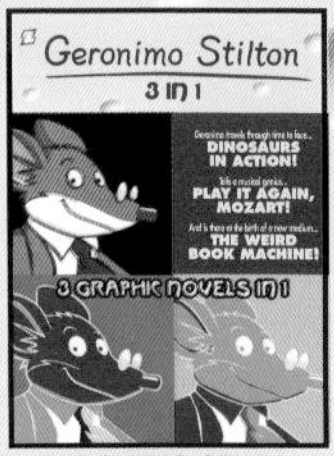
GERONIMO STILTON 3 in 1 #3

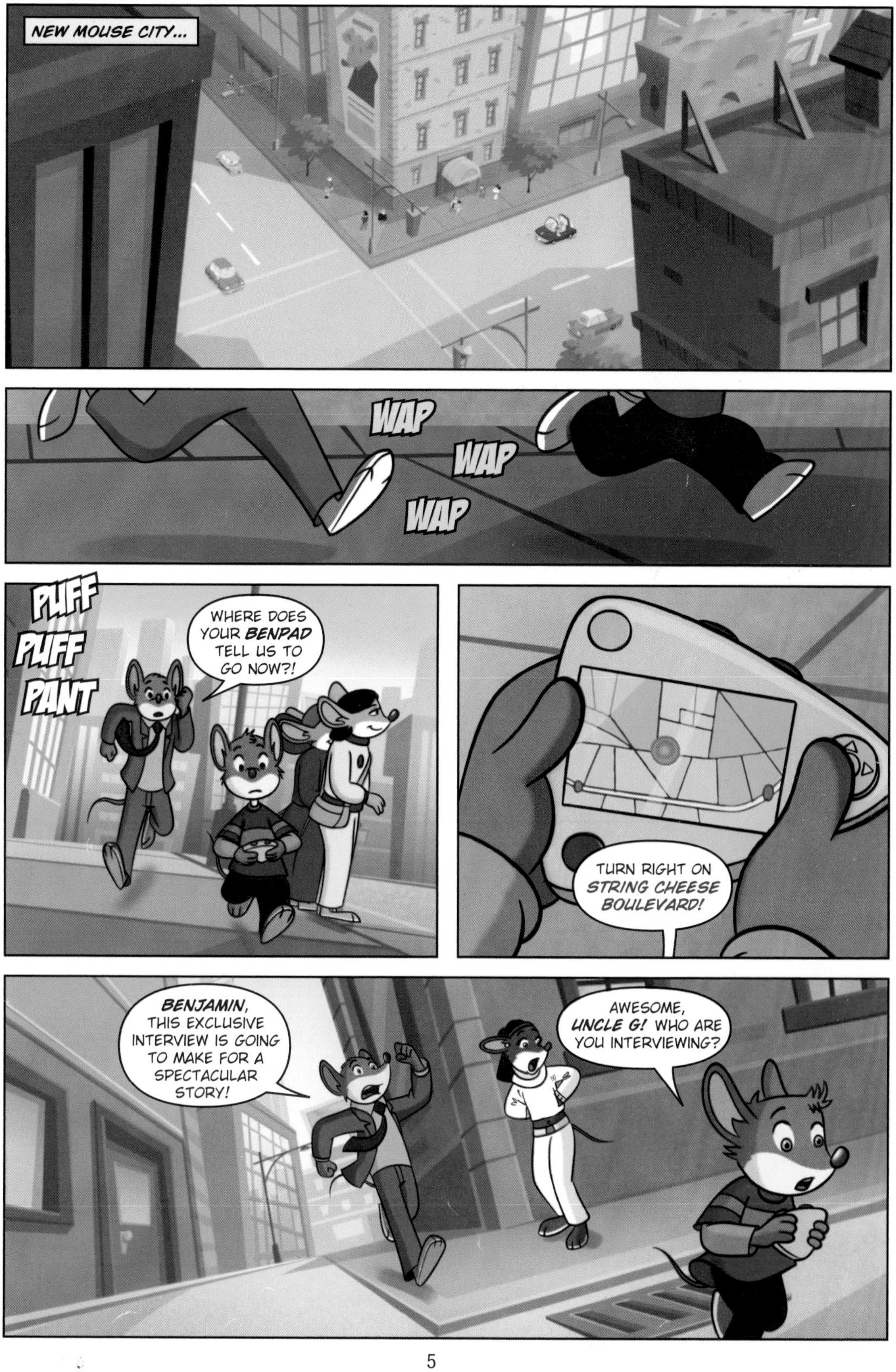
NEW MOUSE CITY...
WAP
WAP
WAP
PUFF
PUFF
PANT
WHERE DOES YOUR BENPAD TELL US TO GO NOW?!
TURN RIGHT ON STRING CHEESE BOULEVARD!
BENJAMIN, THIS EXCLUSIVE INTERVIEW IS GOING TO MAKE FOR A SPECTACULAR STORY!
AWESOME, UNCLE G! WHO ARE YOU INTERVIEWING?

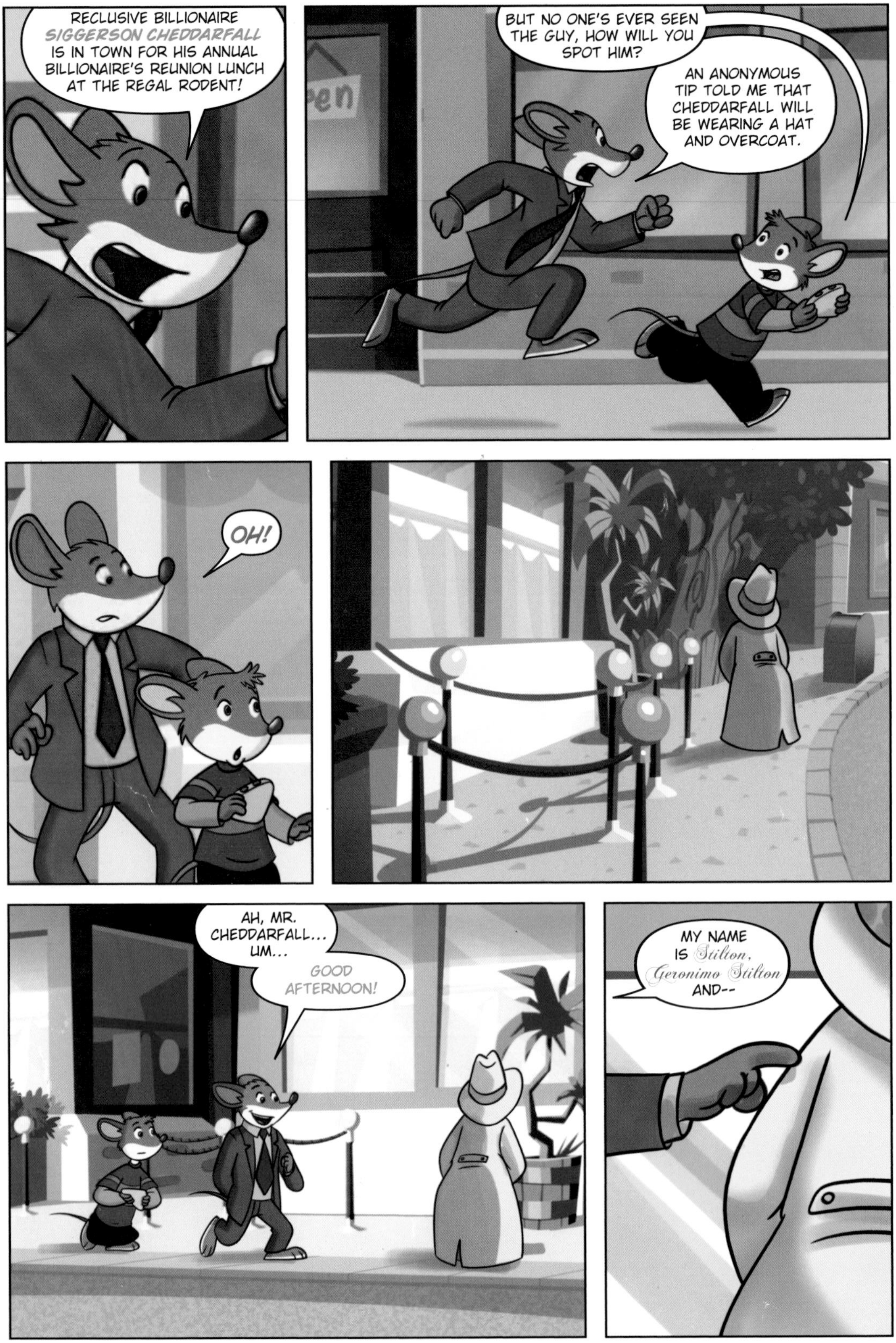
RECLUSIVE BILLIONAIRE SIGGERSON CHEDDARFALL IS IN TOWN FOR HIS ANNUAL BILLIONAIRE'S REUNION LUNCH AT THE REGAL RODENT!
BUT NO ONE'S EVER SEEN THE GUY, HOW WILL YOU SPOT HIM?
AN ANONYMOUS TIP TOLD ME THAT CHEDDARFALL WILL BE WEARING A HAT AND OVERCOAT.
OH!
AH, MR. CHEDDARFALL... UM...
GOOD AFTERNOON!
MY NAME IS Stilton, Geronimo Stilton AND--

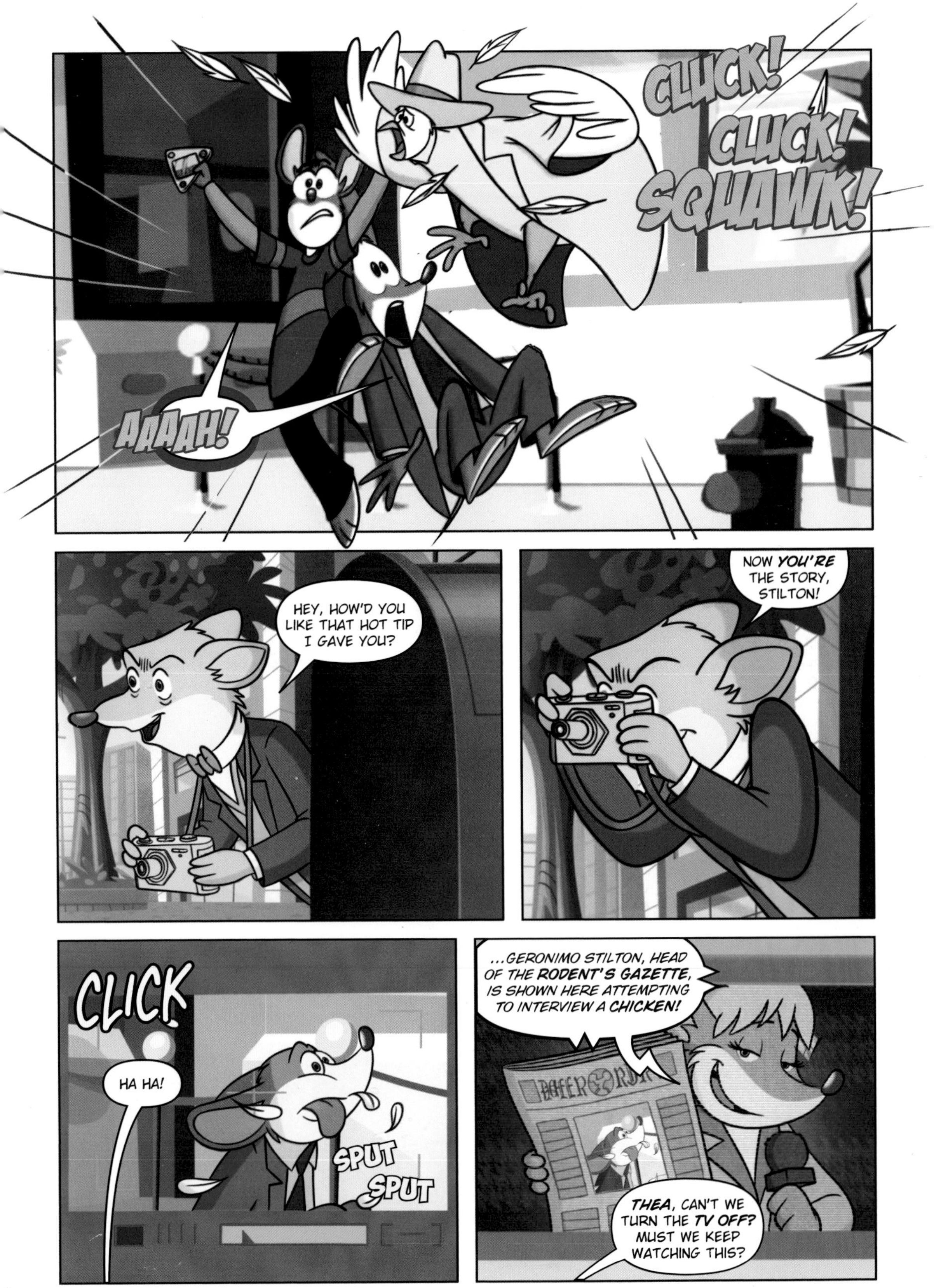
CLUCK! CLUCK! SQUAWK!
AAAAH!
HEY, HOW'D YOU LIKE THAT HOT TIP I GAVE YOU?
NOW YOU'RE THE STORY, STILTON!
CLICK
HA HA!
SPUT
SPUT
...GERONIMO STILTON, HEAD OF THE RODENT'S GAZETTE, IS SHOWN HERE ATTEMPTING TO INTERVIEW A CHICKEN!
THEA, CAN'T WE TURN THE TV OFF? MUST WE KEEP WATCHING THIS?

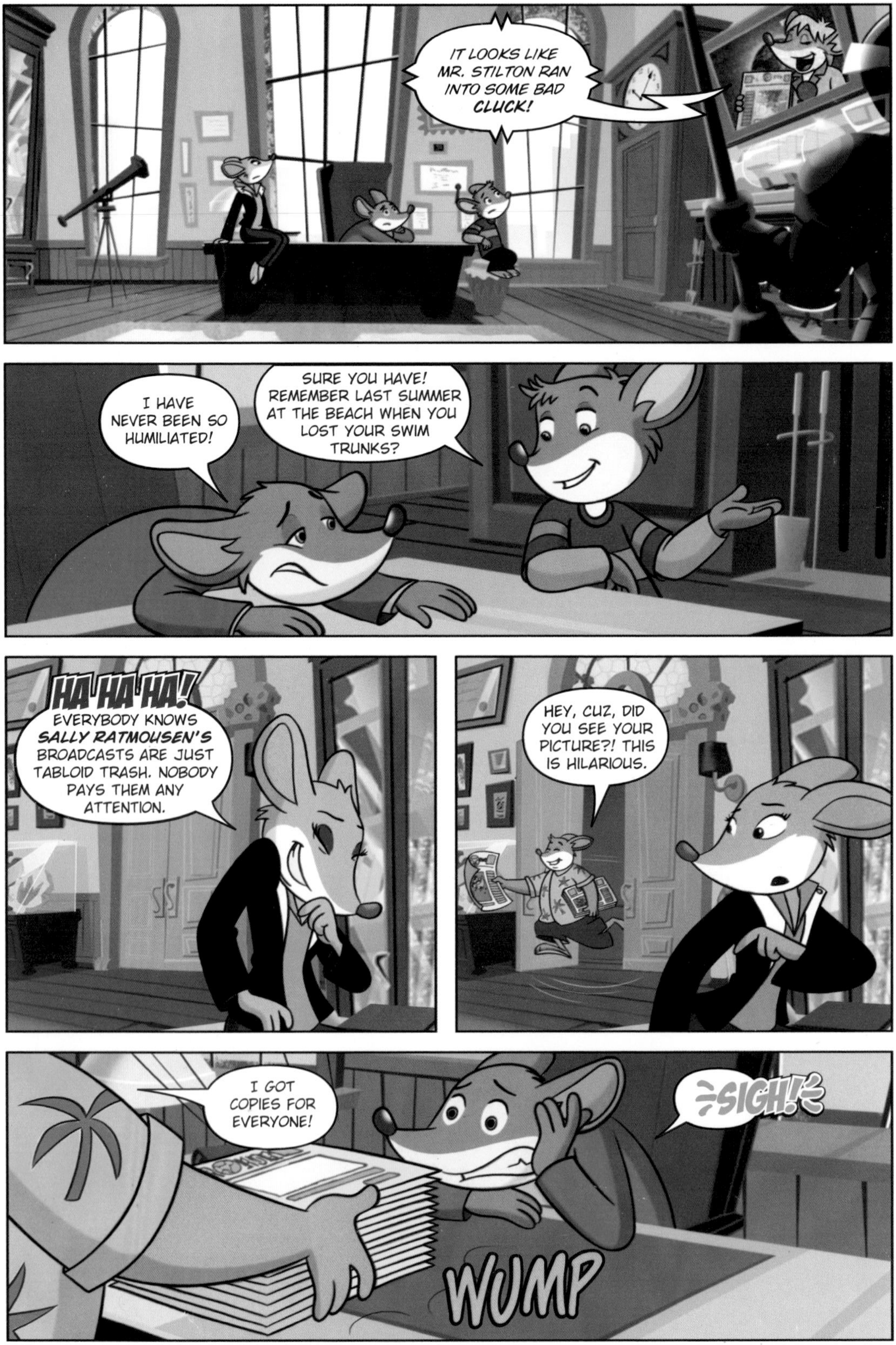
IT LOOKS LIKE MR. STILTON RAN INTO SOME BAD CLUCK!
I HAVE NEVER BEEN SO HUMILIATED!
SURE YOU HAVE! REMEMBER LAST SUMMER AT THE BEACH WHEN YOU LOST YOUR SWIM TRUNKS?
HA HA HA!
EVERYBODY KNOWS SALLY RATMOUSEN'S BROADCASTS ARE JUST TABLOID TRASH. NOBODY PAYS THEM ANY ATTENTION.
HEY, CUZ, DID YOU SEE YOUR PICTURE?! THIS IS HILARIOUS.
I GOT COPIES FOR EVERYONE!
SIGH!
WUMP

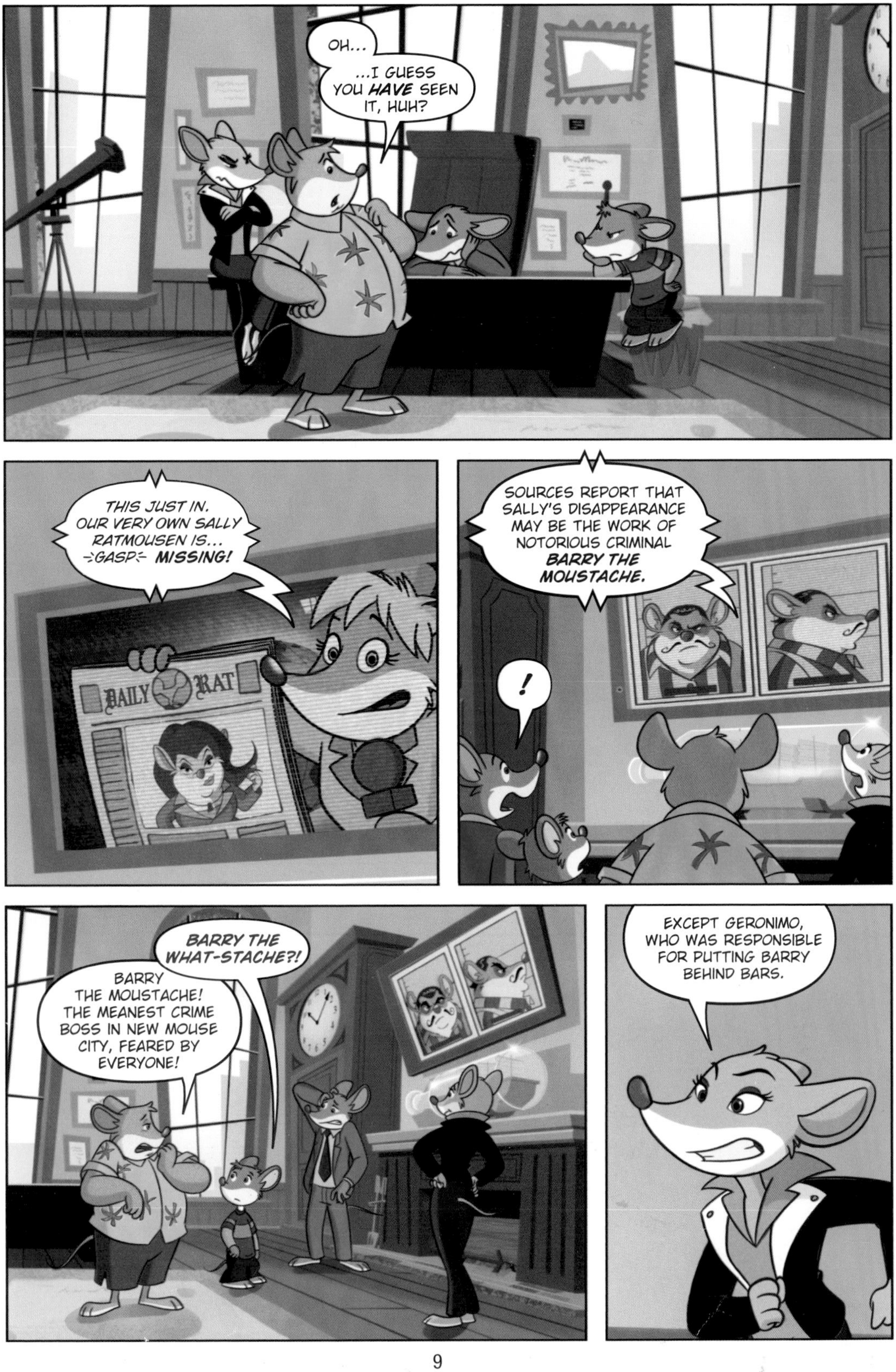
OH...
...I GUESS YOU HAVE SEEN IT, HUH?
THIS JUST IN. OUR VERY OWN SALLY RATMOUSEN IS... GASP MISSING!
DAILY RAT
SOURCES REPORT THAT SALLY'S DISAPPEARANCE MAY BE THE WORK OF NOTORIOUS CRIMINAL BARRY THE MOUSTACHE.
!
BARRY THE MOUSTACHE! THE MEANEST CRIME BOSS IN NEW MOUSE CITY, FEARED BY EVERYONE!
BARRY THE WHAT-STACHE?!
EXCEPT GERONIMO, WHO WAS RESPONSIBLE FOR PUTTING BARRY BEHIND BARS.

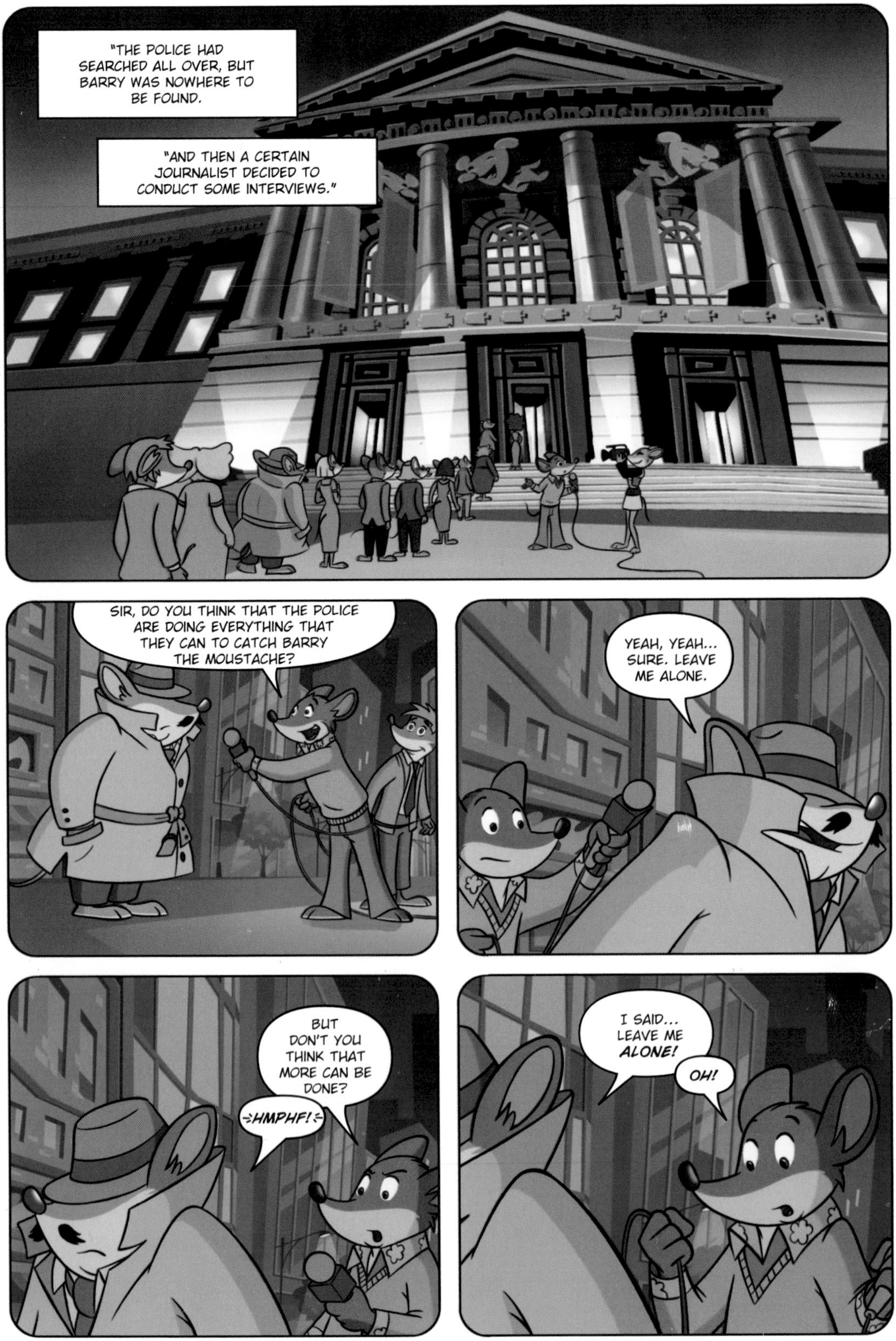
"THE POLICE HAD SEARCHED ALL OVER, BUT BARRY WAS NOWHERE TO BE FOUND.
"AND THEN A CERTAIN JOURNALIST DECIDED TO CONDUCT SOME INTERVIEWS."
SIR, DO YOU THINK THAT THE POLICE ARE DOING EVERYTHING THAT THEY CAN TO CATCH BARRY THE MOUSTACHE?
YEAH, YEAH... SURE. LEAVE ME ALONE.
BUT DON'T YOU THINK THAT MORE CAN BE DONE?
HMPHF!
I SAID... LEAVE ME ALONE!
OH!

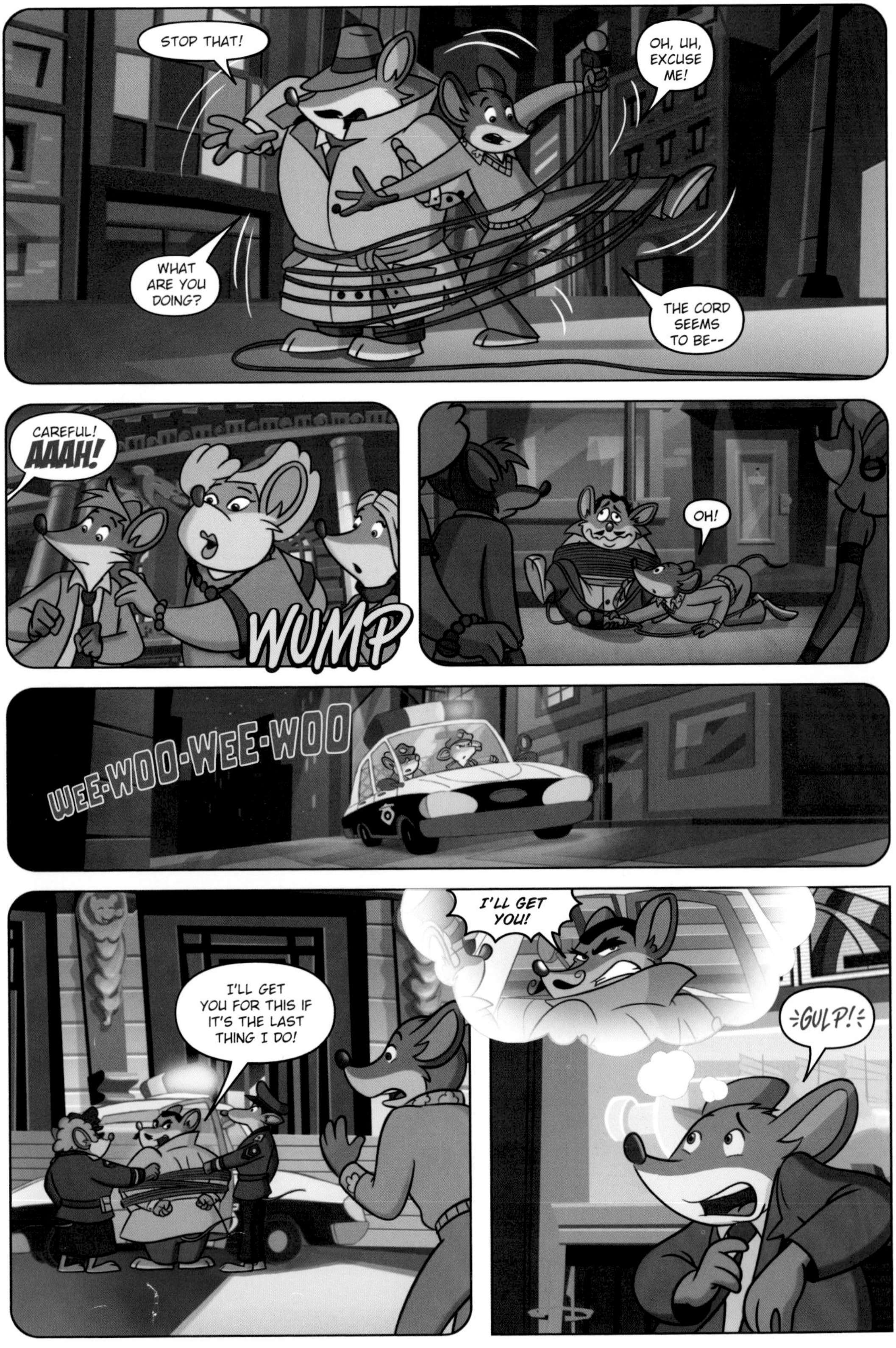
STOP THAT!
OH, UH, EXCUSE ME!
WHAT ARE YOU DOING?
THE CORD SEEMS TO BE--
CAREFUL!
AAAH!
WUMP
OH!
WEE-WOO-WEE-WOO
I'LL GET YOU FOR THIS IF IT'S THE LAST THING I DO!
I'LL GET YOU!
GULP!

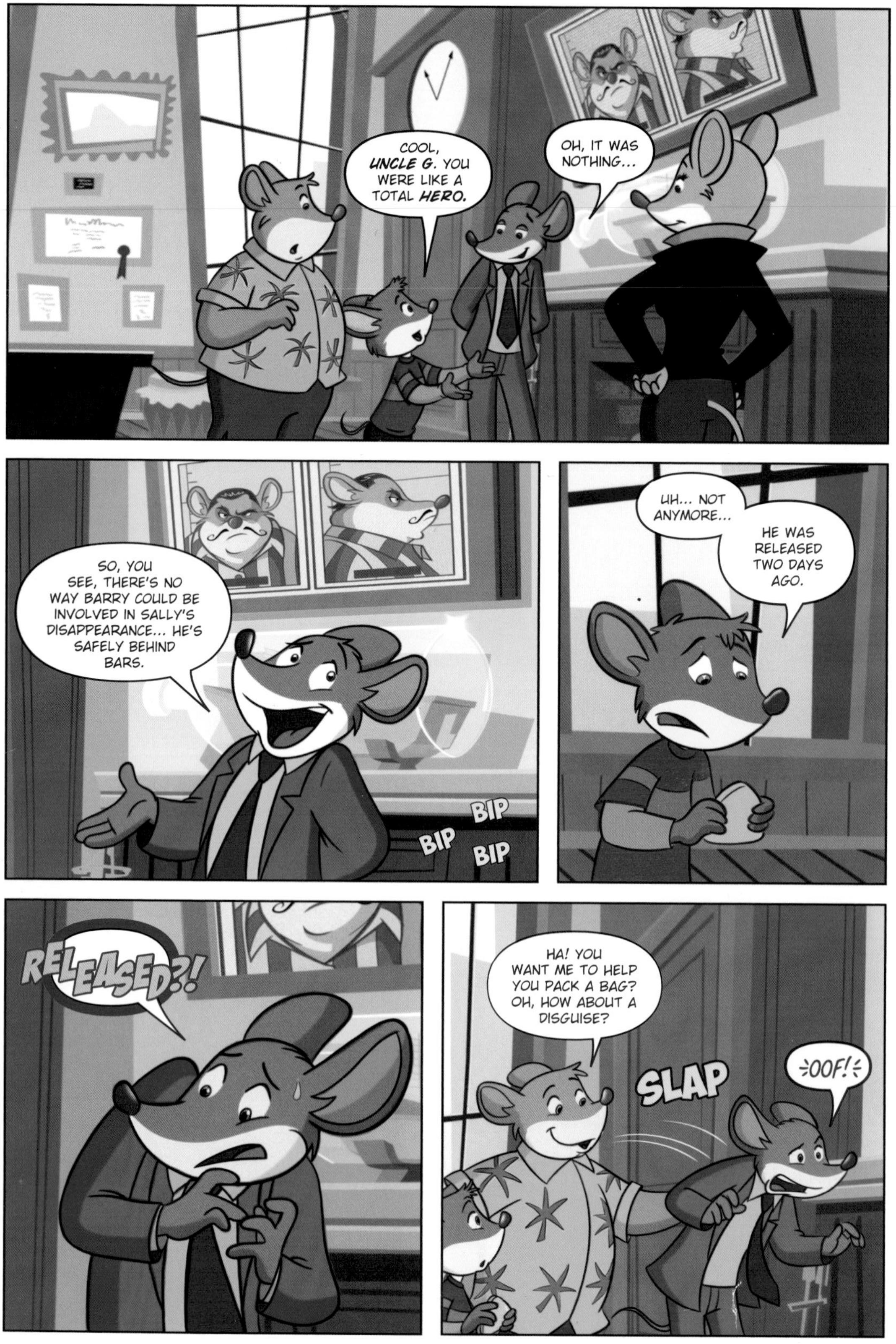

COOL, UNCLE G. YOU WERE LIKE A TOTAL HERO.
OH, IT WAS NOTHING...
SO, YOU SEE, THERE'S NO WAY BARRY COULD BE INVOLVED IN SALLY'S DISAPPEARANCE... HE'S SAFELY BEHIND BARS.
BIP
BIP
BIP
UH... NOT ANYMORE...
HE WAS RELEASED TWO DAYS AGO.
RELEASED?!
HA! YOU WANT ME TO HELP YOU PACK A BAG? OH, HOW ABOUT A DISGUISE?
SLAP
OOF!

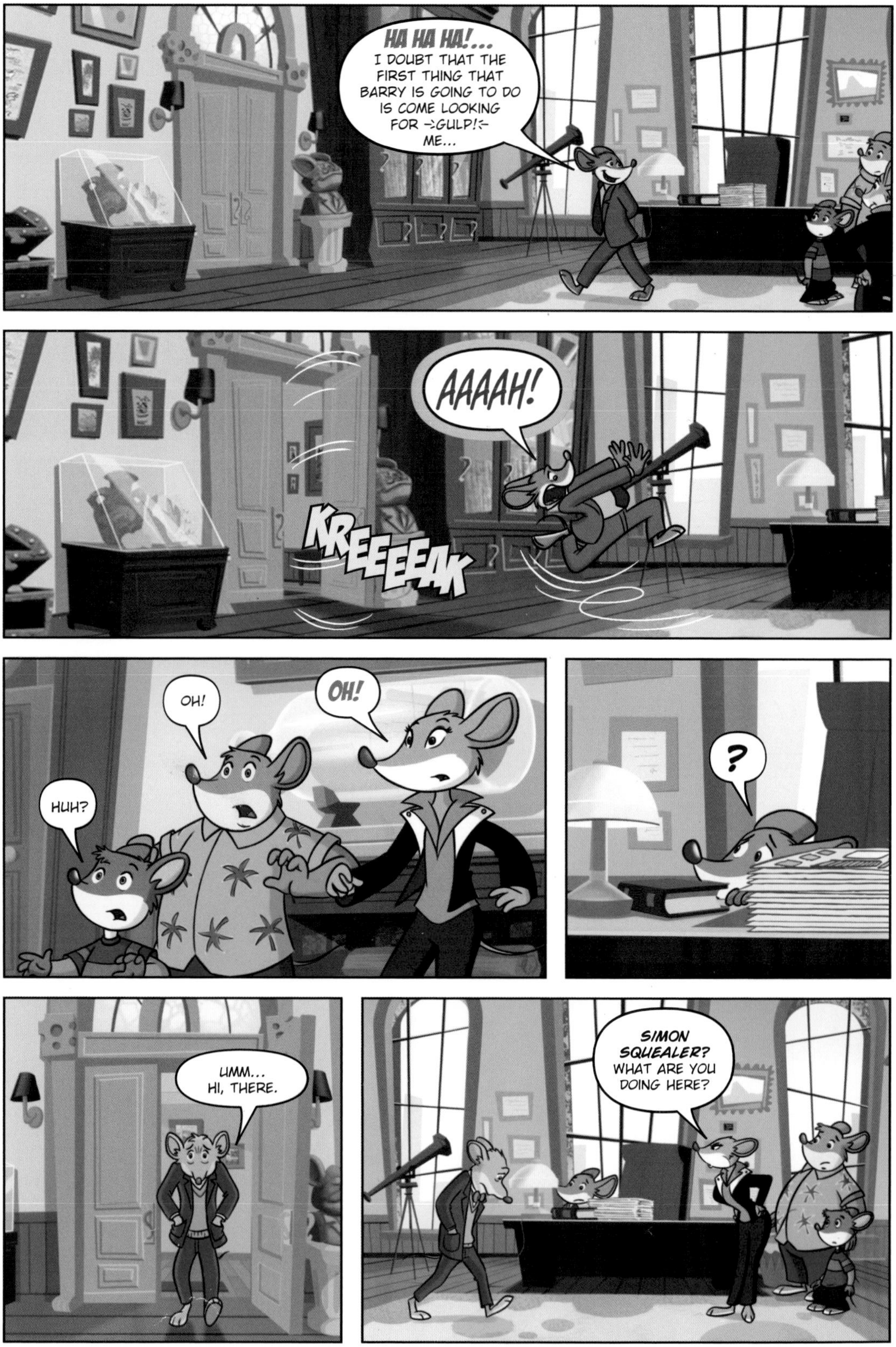
HA HA HA!...
I DOUBT THAT THE FIRST THING THAT BARRY IS GOING TO DO IS COME LOOKING FOR ->GULP!<- ME...
AAAAH!
KREEEEAK
HUH?
OH!
OH!
?
UMM... HI, THERE.
SIMON SQUEALER? WHAT ARE YOU DOING HERE?

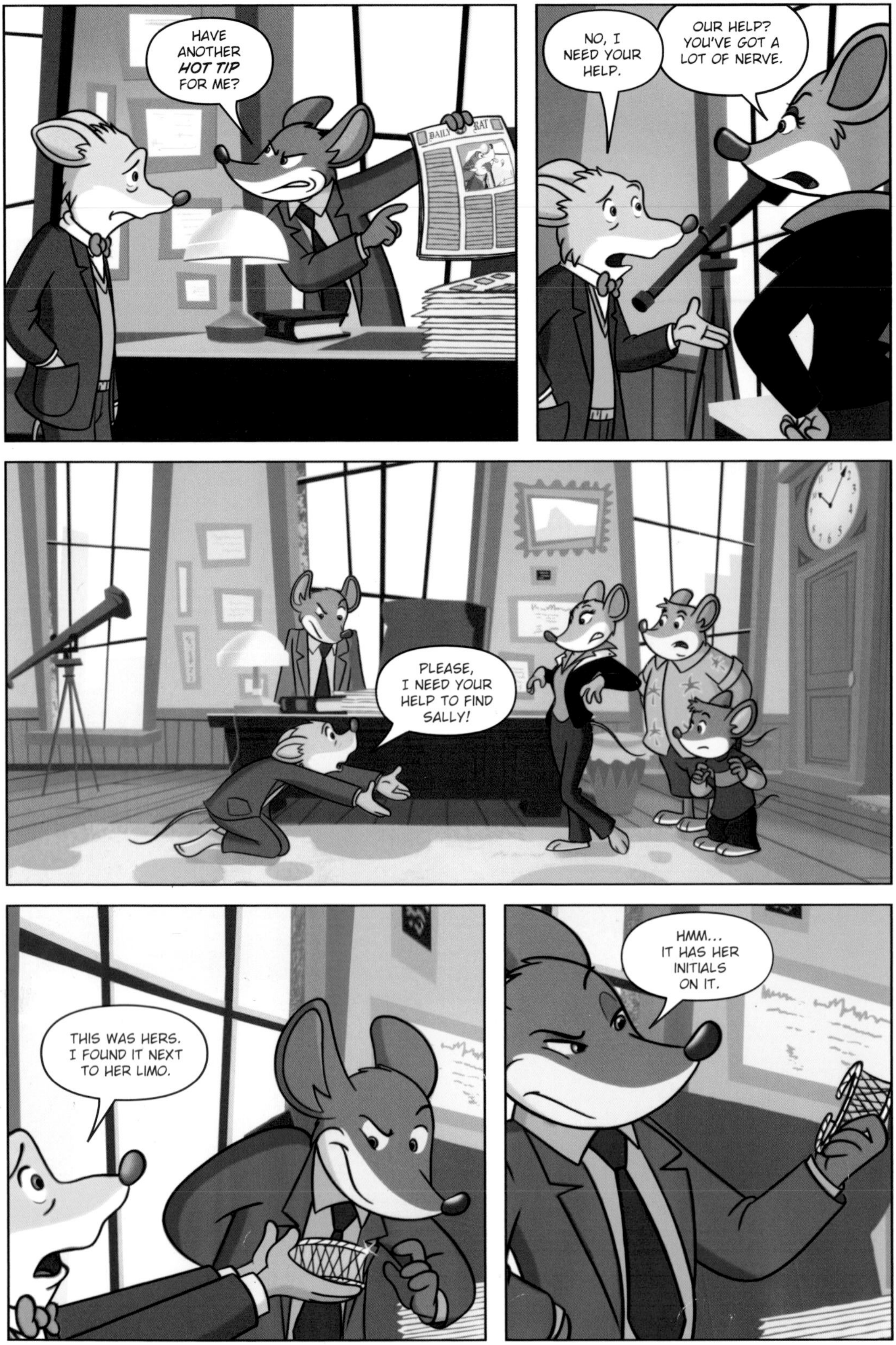
HAVE ANOTHER ***HOT TIP*** FOR ME?
DAILY RAT
NO, I NEED YOUR HELP.
OUR HELP? YOU'VE GOT A LOT OF NERVE.
PLEASE, I NEED YOUR HELP TO FIND SALLY!
THIS WAS HERS. I FOUND IT NEXT TO HER LIMO.
HMM... IT HAS HER INITIALS ON IT.

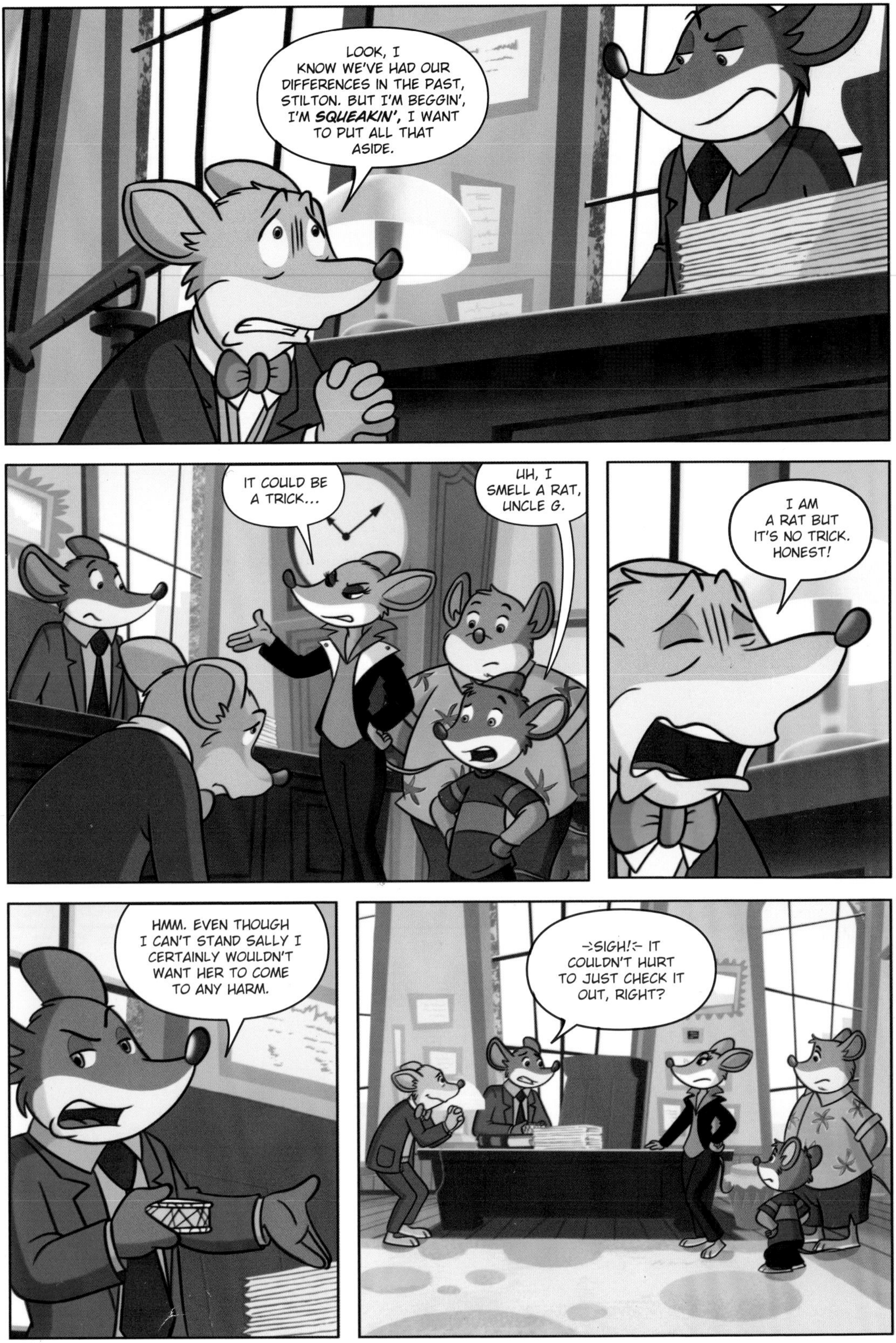
LOOK, I KNOW WE'VE HAD OUR DIFFERENCES IN THE PAST, STILTON. BUT I'M BEGGIN', I'M **SQUEAKIN'**, I WANT TO PUT ALL THAT ASIDE.
IT COULD BE A TRICK...
UH, I SMELL A RAT, UNCLE G.
I AM A RAT BUT IT'S NO TRICK. HONEST!
HMM. EVEN THOUGH I CAN'T STAND SALLY I CERTAINLY WOULDN'T WANT HER TO COME TO ANY HARM.
-SIGH!- IT COULDN'T HURT TO JUST CHECK IT OUT, RIGHT?

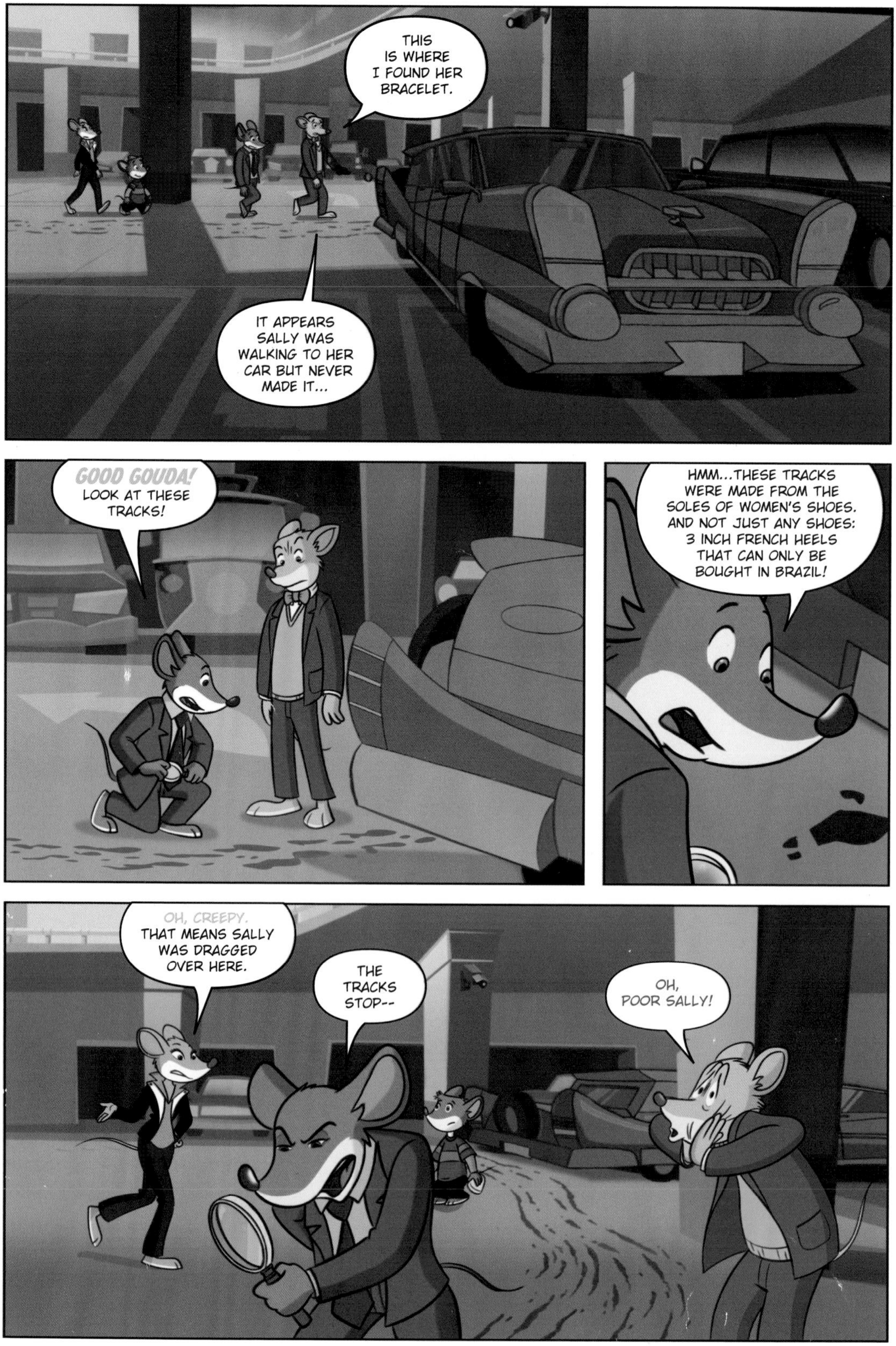
THIS IS WHERE I FOUND HER BRACELET.
IT APPEARS SALLY WAS WALKING TO HER CAR BUT NEVER MADE IT...
GOOD GOUDA! LOOK AT THESE TRACKS!
HMM...THESE TRACKS WERE MADE FROM THE SOLES OF WOMEN'S SHOES. AND NOT JUST ANY SHOES: 3 INCH FRENCH HEELS THAT CAN ONLY BE BOUGHT IN BRAZIL!
OH, CREEPY. THAT MEANS SALLY WAS DRAGGED OVER HERE.
THE TRACKS STOP--
OH, POOR SALLY!

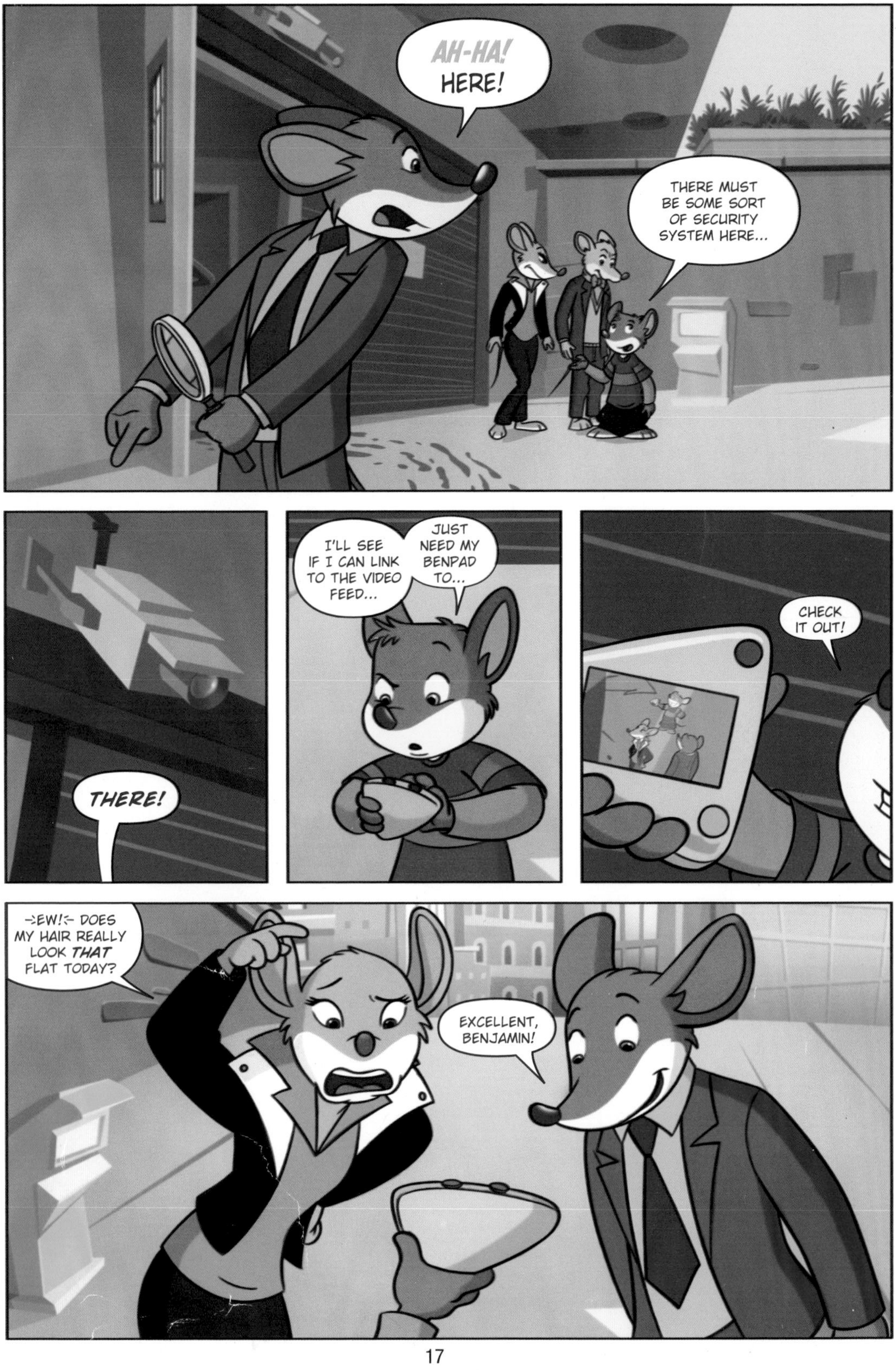
AH-HA! HERE!
THERE MUST BE SOME SORT OF SECURITY SYSTEM HERE...
THERE!
I'LL SEE IF I CAN LINK TO THE VIDEO FEED...
JUST NEED MY BENPAD TO...
CHECK IT OUT!
-EW!- DOES MY HAIR REALLY LOOK *THAT* FLAT TODAY?
EXCELLENT, BENJAMIN!

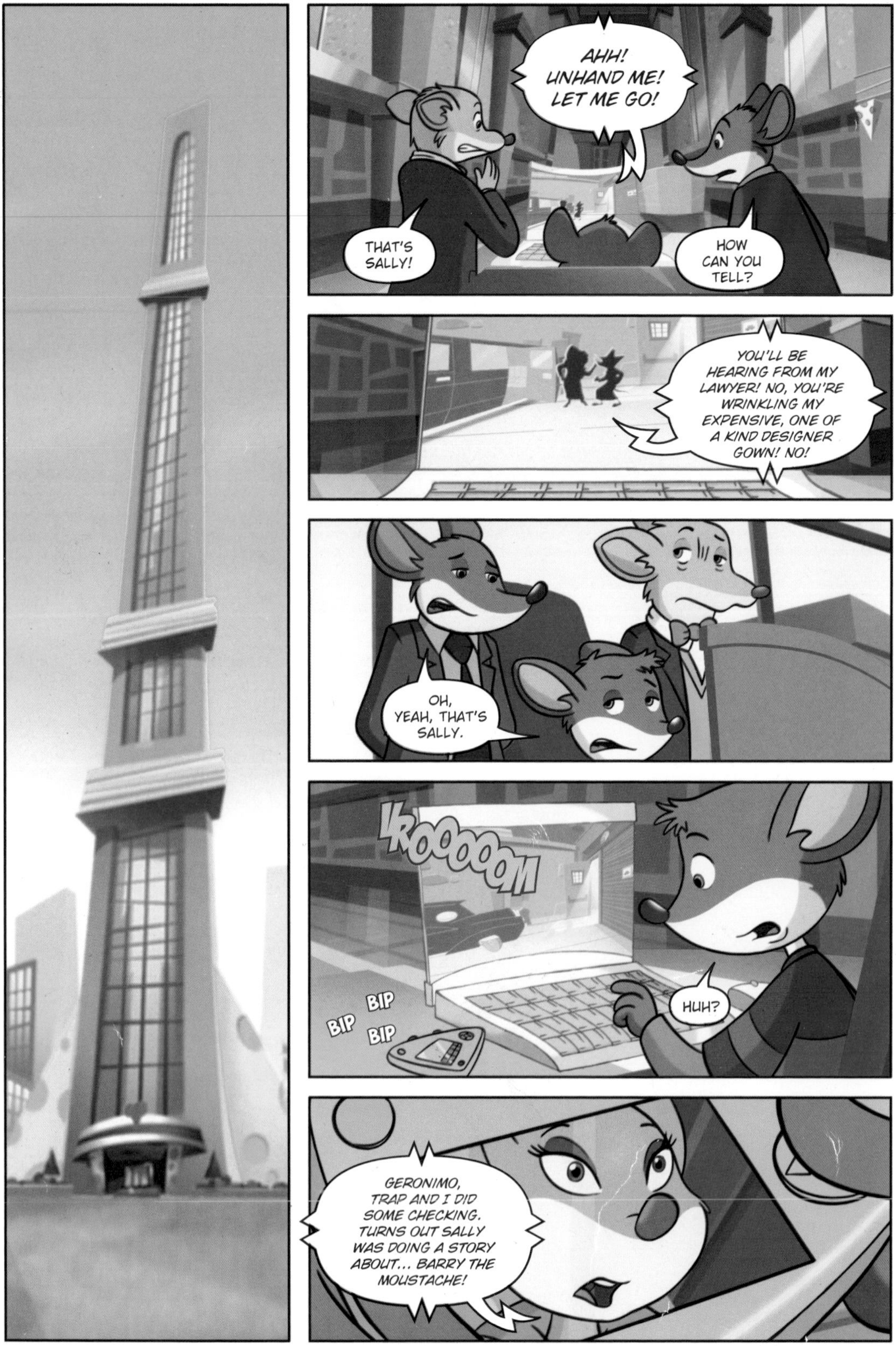
AHH! UNHAND ME! LET ME GO!
THAT'S SALLY!
HOW CAN YOU TELL?
YOU'LL BE HEARING FROM MY LAWYER! NO, YOU'RE WRINKLING MY EXPENSIVE, ONE OF A KIND DESIGNER GOWN! NO!
OH, YEAH, THAT'S SALLY.
VROOOOOM
BIP
BIP
BIP
HUH?
GERONIMO, TRAP AND I DID SOME CHECKING. TURNS OUT SALLY WAS DOING A STORY ABOUT... BARRY THE MOUSTACHE!

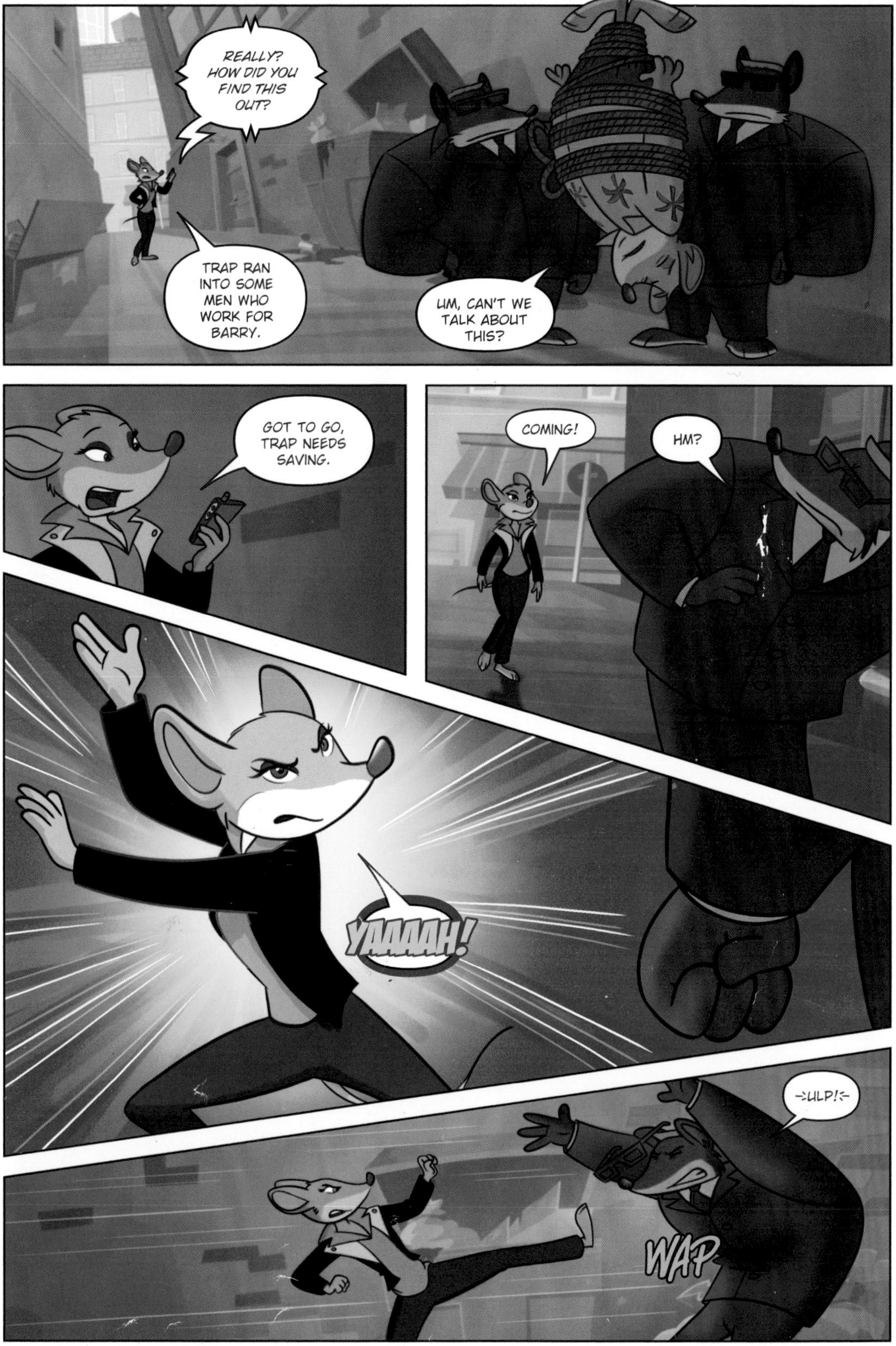
REALLY? HOW DID YOU FIND THIS OUT?
TRAP RAN INTO SOME MEN WHO WORK FOR BARRY.
UM, CAN'T WE TALK ABOUT THIS?
GOT TO GO, TRAP NEEDS SAVING.
COMING!
HM?
YAAAAH!
ULP!
WAP

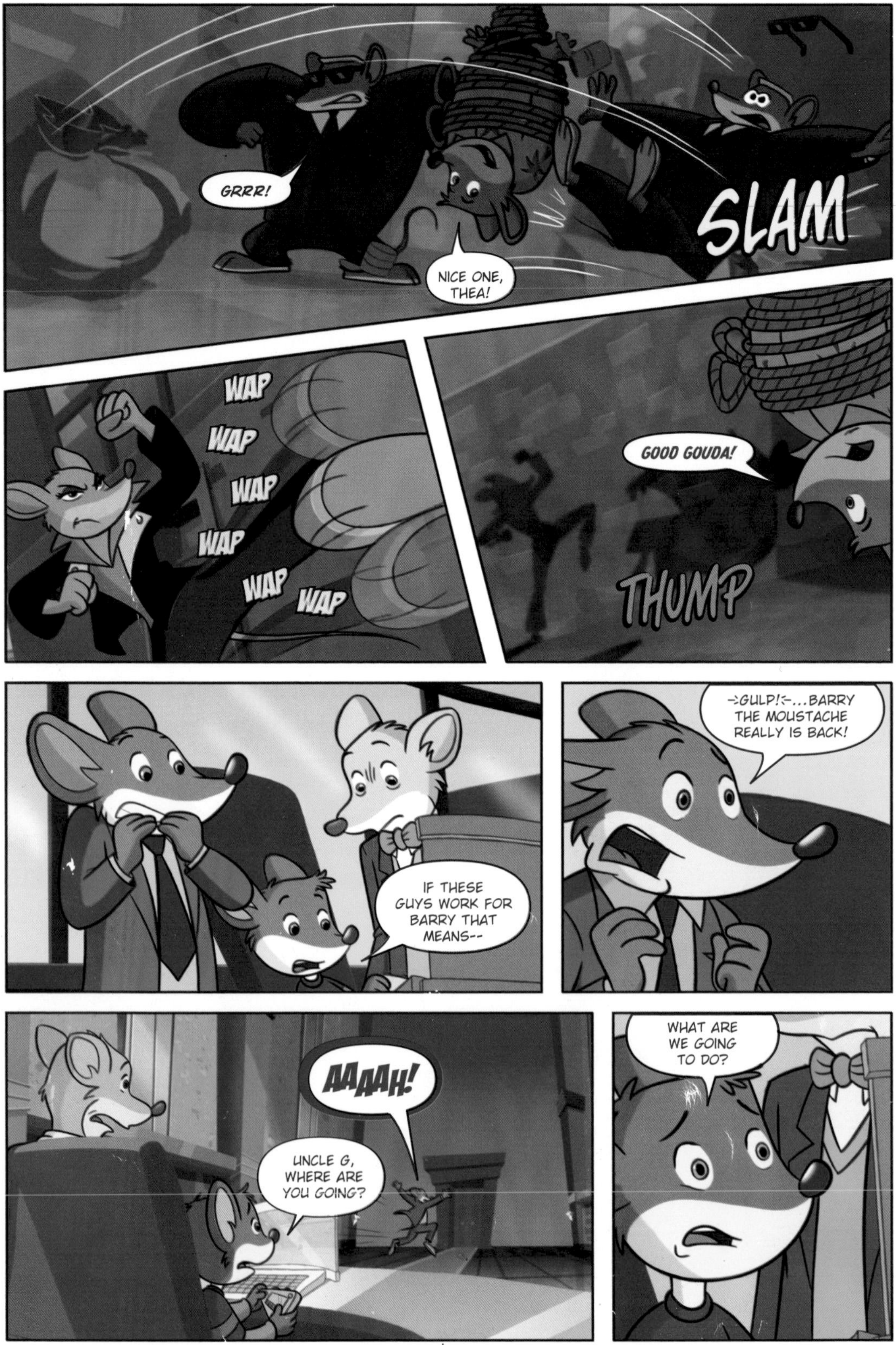
GRRR!
NICE ONE, THEA!
SLAM
WAP
WAP
WAP
WAP
WAP
WAP
GOOD GOUDA!
THUMP
IF THESE GUYS WORK FOR BARRY THAT MEANS--
-GULP!- ...BARRY THE MOUSTACHE REALLY IS BACK!
AAAAH!
UNCLE G, WHERE ARE YOU GOING?
WHAT ARE WE GOING TO DO?

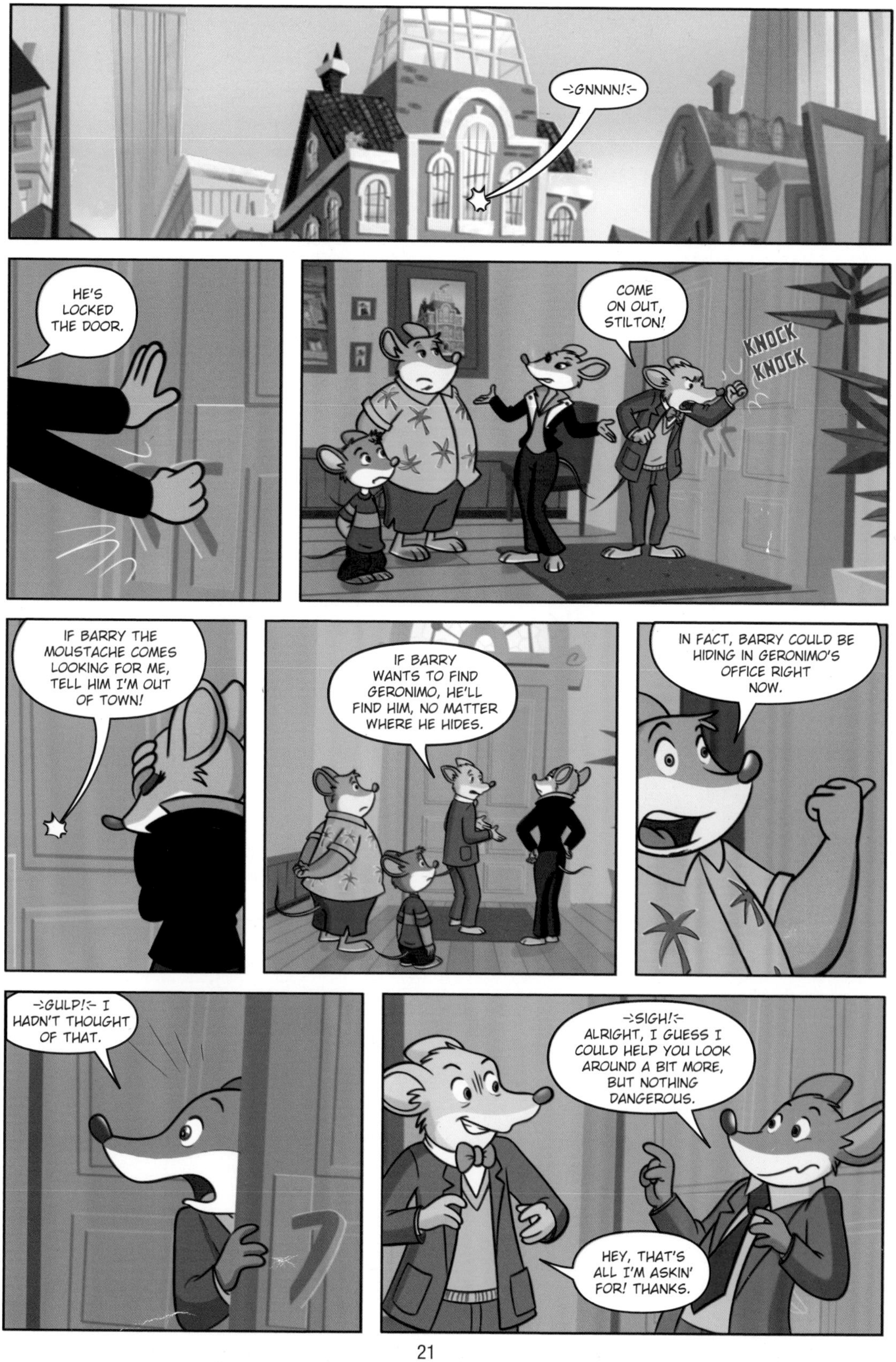

–GNNNN!–
HE'S LOCKED THE DOOR.
COME ON OUT, STILTON!
KNOCK KNOCK
IF BARRY THE MOUSTACHE COMES LOOKING FOR ME, TELL HIM I'M OUT OF TOWN!
IF BARRY WANTS TO FIND GERONIMO, HE'LL FIND HIM, NO MATTER WHERE HE HIDES.
IN FACT, BARRY COULD BE HIDING IN GERONIMO'S OFFICE RIGHT NOW.
–GULP!– I HADN'T THOUGHT OF THAT.
–SIGH!– ALRIGHT, I GUESS I COULD HELP YOU LOOK AROUND A BIT MORE, BUT NOTHING DANGEROUS.
HEY, THAT'S ALL I'M ASKIN' FOR! THANKS.

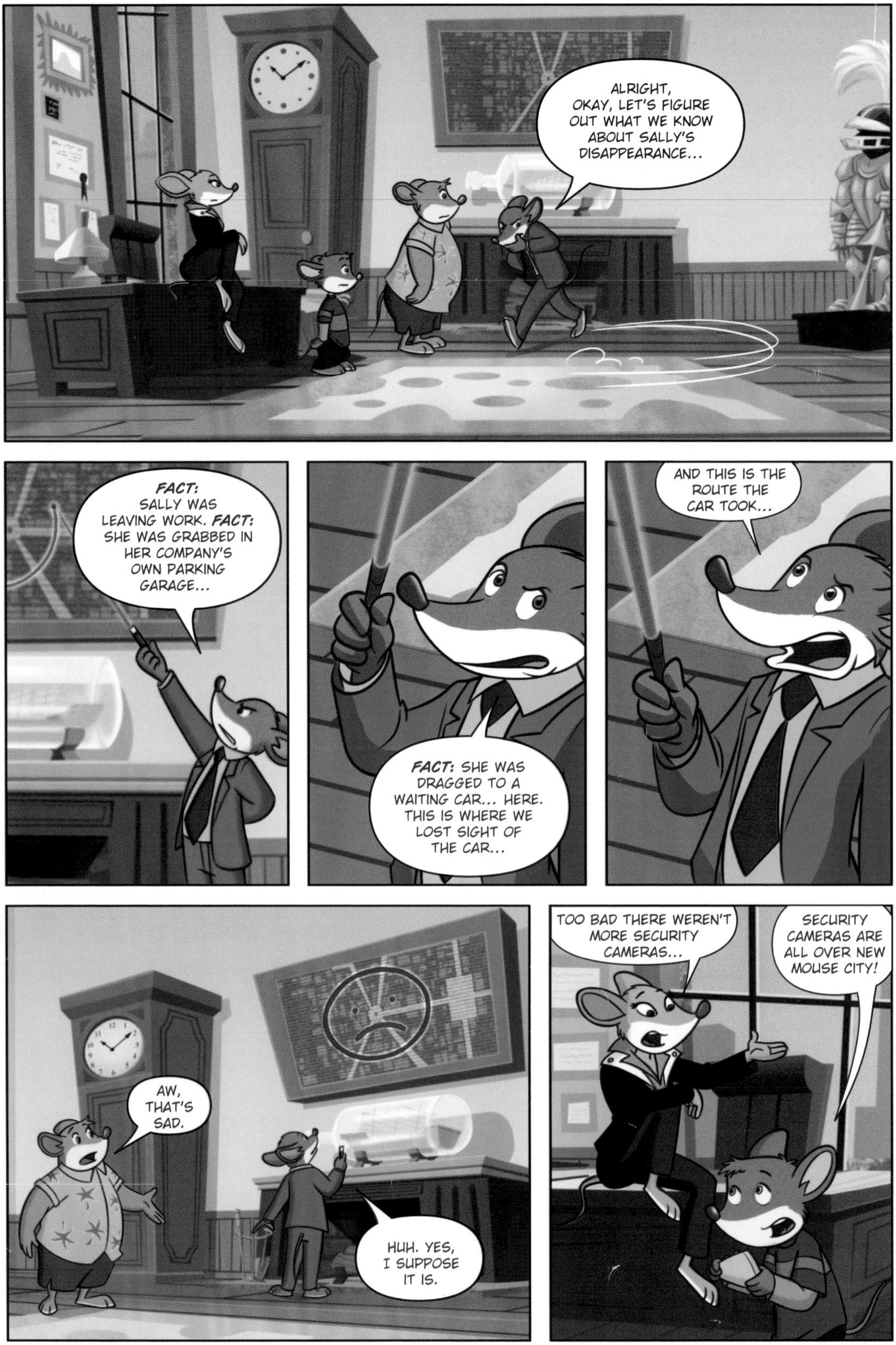
ALRIGHT, OKAY, LET'S FIGURE OUT WHAT WE KNOW ABOUT SALLY'S DISAPPEARANCE...
FACT: SALLY WAS LEAVING WORK. FACT: SHE WAS GRABBED IN HER COMPANY'S OWN PARKING GARAGE...
FACT: SHE WAS DRAGGED TO A WAITING CAR... HERE. THIS IS WHERE WE LOST SIGHT OF THE CAR...
AND THIS IS THE ROUTE THE CAR TOOK...
AW, THAT'S SAD.
HUH. YES, I SUPPOSE IT IS.
TOO BAD THERE WEREN'T MORE SECURITY CAMERAS...
SECURITY CAMERAS ARE ALL OVER NEW MOUSE CITY!

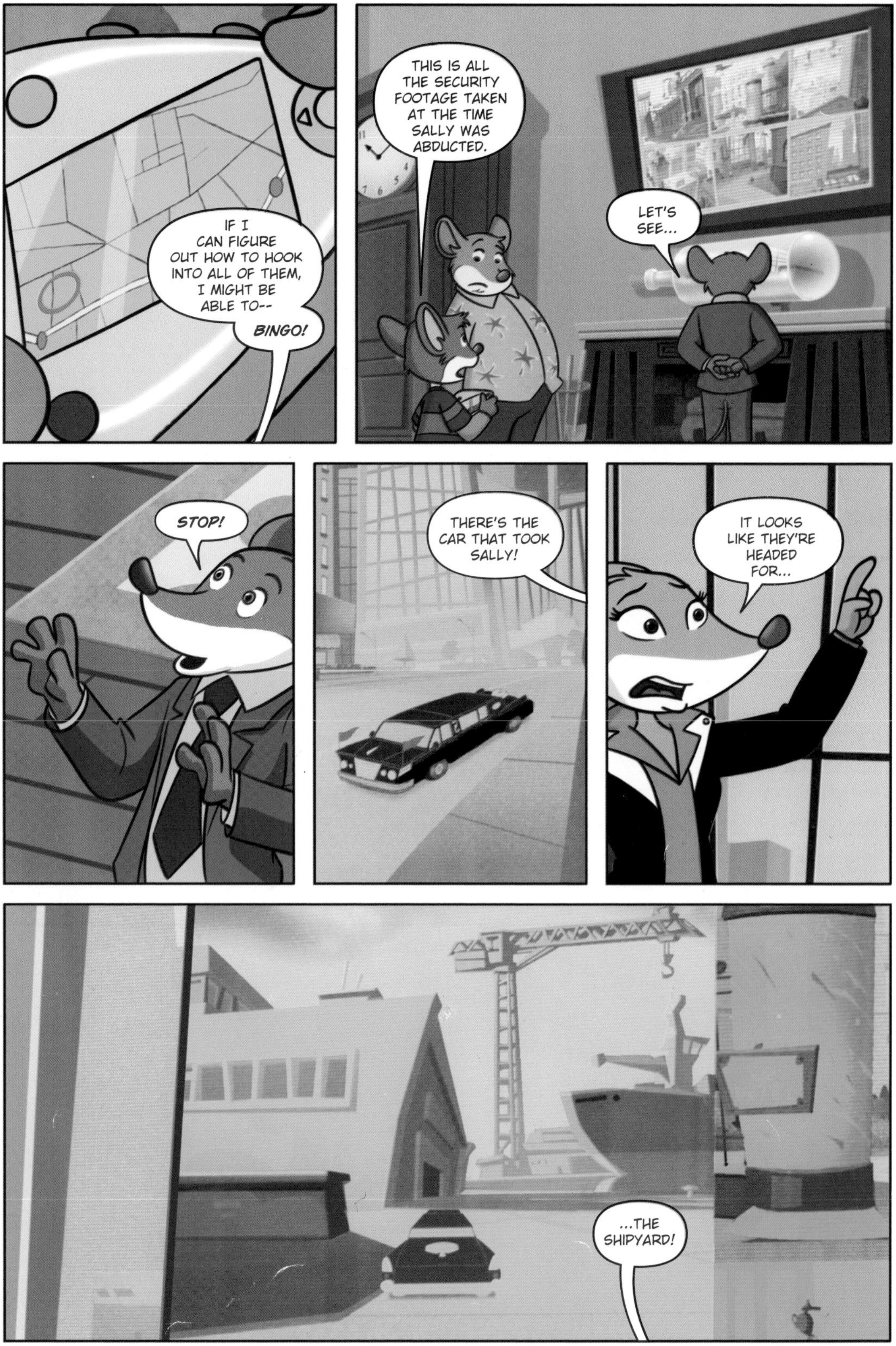
IF I CAN FIGURE OUT HOW TO HOOK INTO ALL OF THEM, I MIGHT BE ABLE TO--
BINGO!
THIS IS ALL THE SECURITY FOOTAGE TAKEN AT THE TIME SALLY WAS ABDUCTED.
LET'S SEE...
STOP!
THERE'S THE CAR THAT TOOK SALLY!
IT LOOKS LIKE THEY'RE HEADED FOR...
...THE SHIPYARD!

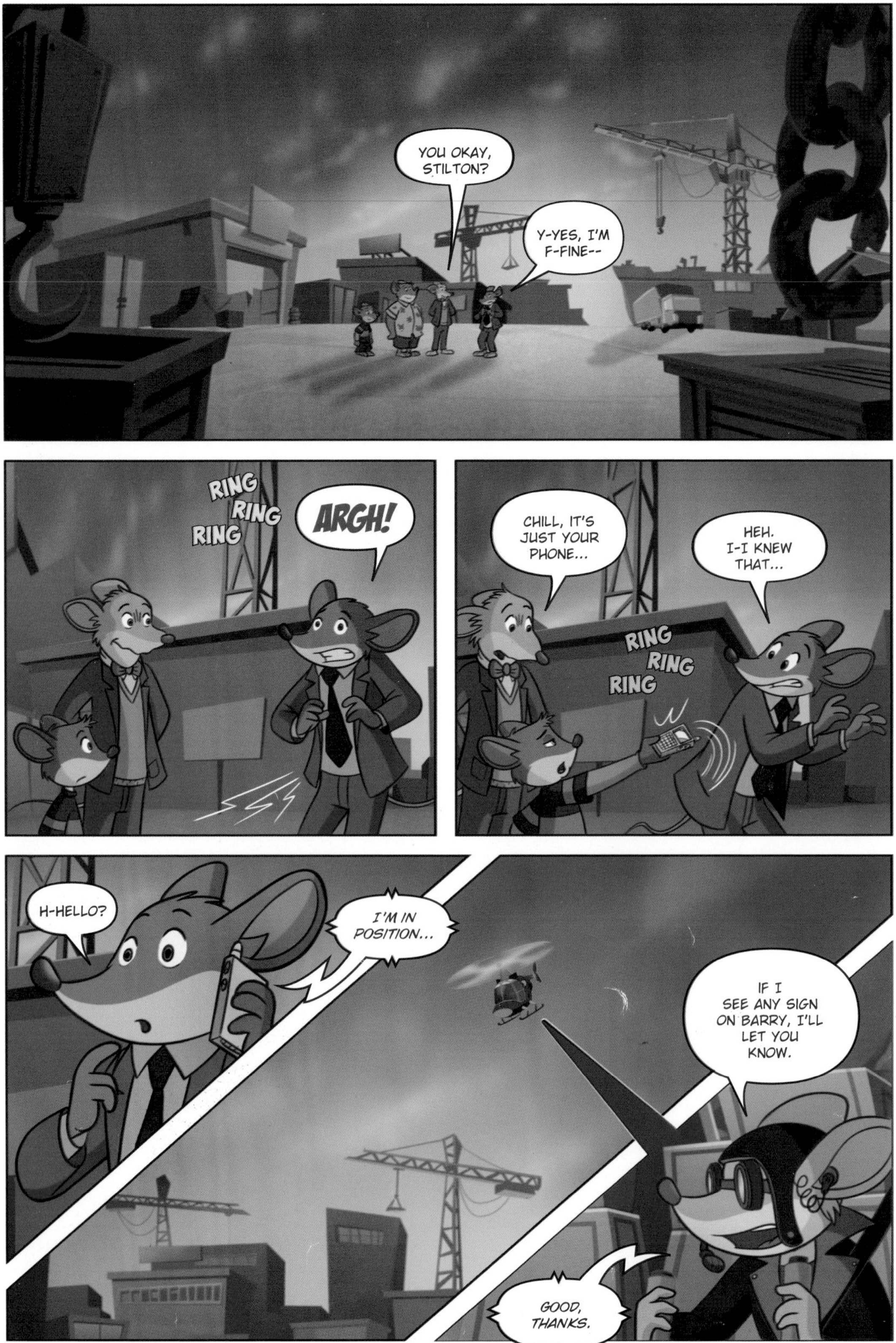
YOU OKAY, STILTON?
Y-YES, I'M F-FINE--
RING RING RING
ARGH!
CHILL, IT'S JUST YOUR PHONE...
HEH. I-I KNEW THAT...
RING RING RING
H-HELLO?
I'M IN POSITION...
IF I SEE ANY SIGN ON BARRY, I'LL LET YOU KNOW.
GOOD, THANKS.

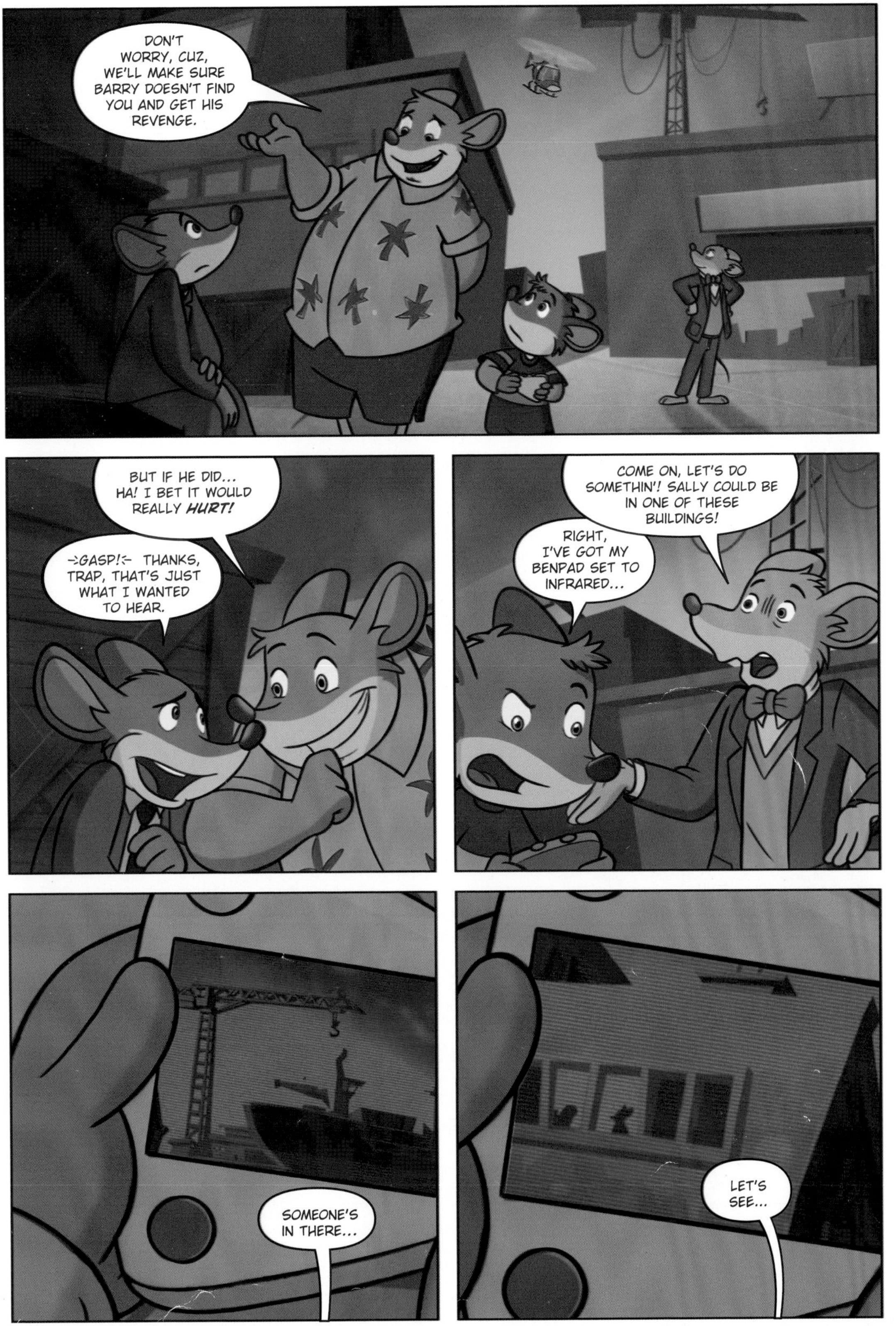
DON'T WORRY, CUZ, WE'LL MAKE SURE BARRY DOESN'T FIND YOU AND GET HIS REVENGE.
BUT IF HE DID... HA! I BET IT WOULD REALLY *HURT!*
-GASP!- THANKS, TRAP, THAT'S JUST WHAT I WANTED TO HEAR.
COME ON, LET'S DO SOMETHIN'! SALLY COULD BE IN ONE OF THESE BUILDINGS!
RIGHT, I'VE GOT MY BENPAD SET TO INFRARED...
SOMEONE'S IN THERE...
LET'S SEE...

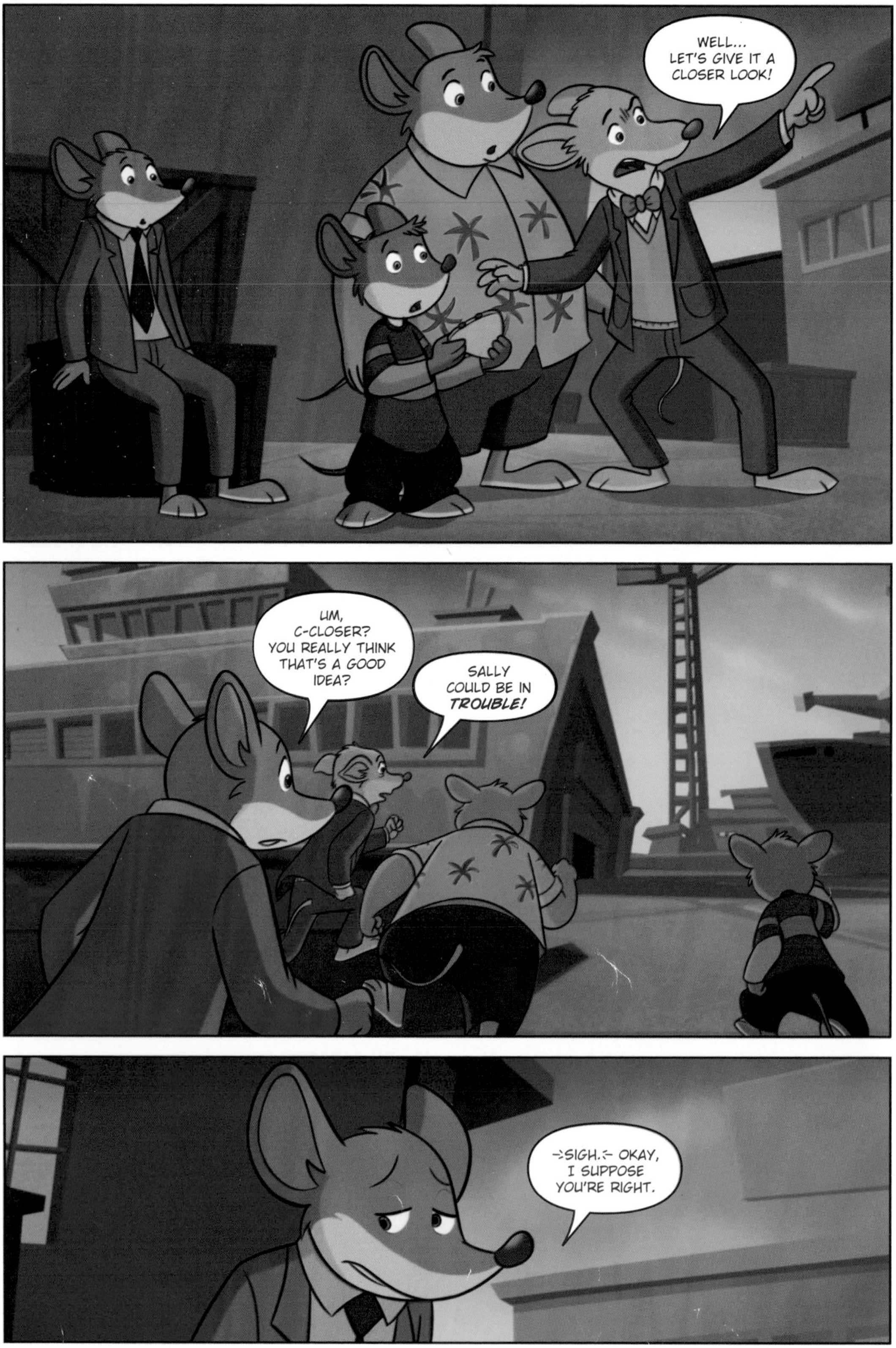
WELL... LET'S GIVE IT A CLOSER LOOK!
UM, C-CLOSER? YOU REALLY THINK THAT'S A GOOD IDEA?
SALLY COULD BE IN *TROUBLE!*
-SIGH.- OKAY, I SUPPOSE YOU'RE RIGHT.

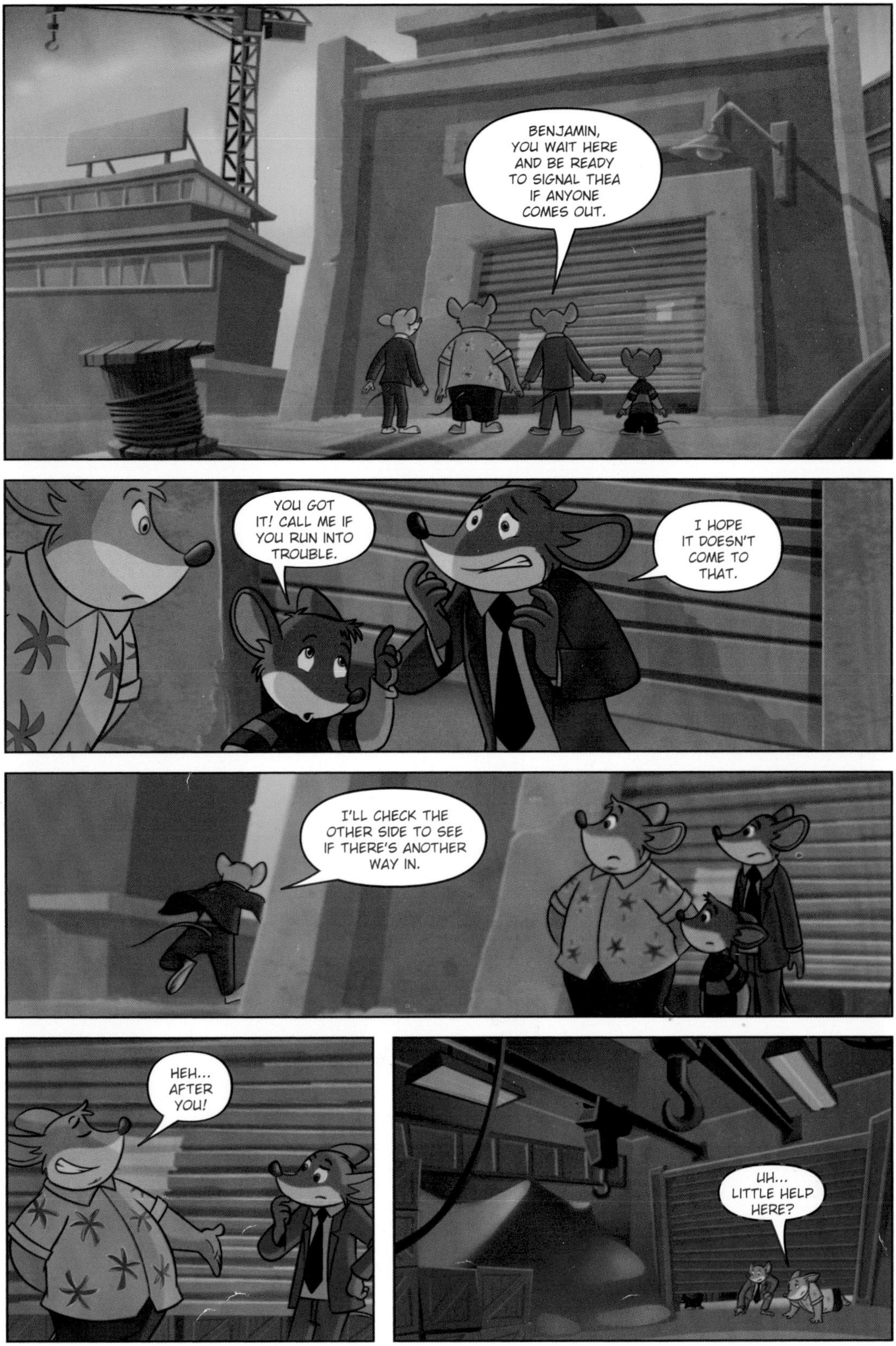
BENJAMIN, YOU WAIT HERE AND BE READY TO SIGNAL THEA IF ANYONE COMES OUT.
YOU GOT IT! CALL ME IF YOU RUN INTO TROUBLE.
I HOPE IT DOESN'T COME TO THAT.
I'LL CHECK THE OTHER SIDE TO SEE IF THERE'S ANOTHER WAY IN.
HEH... AFTER YOU!
UH... LITTLE HELP HERE?

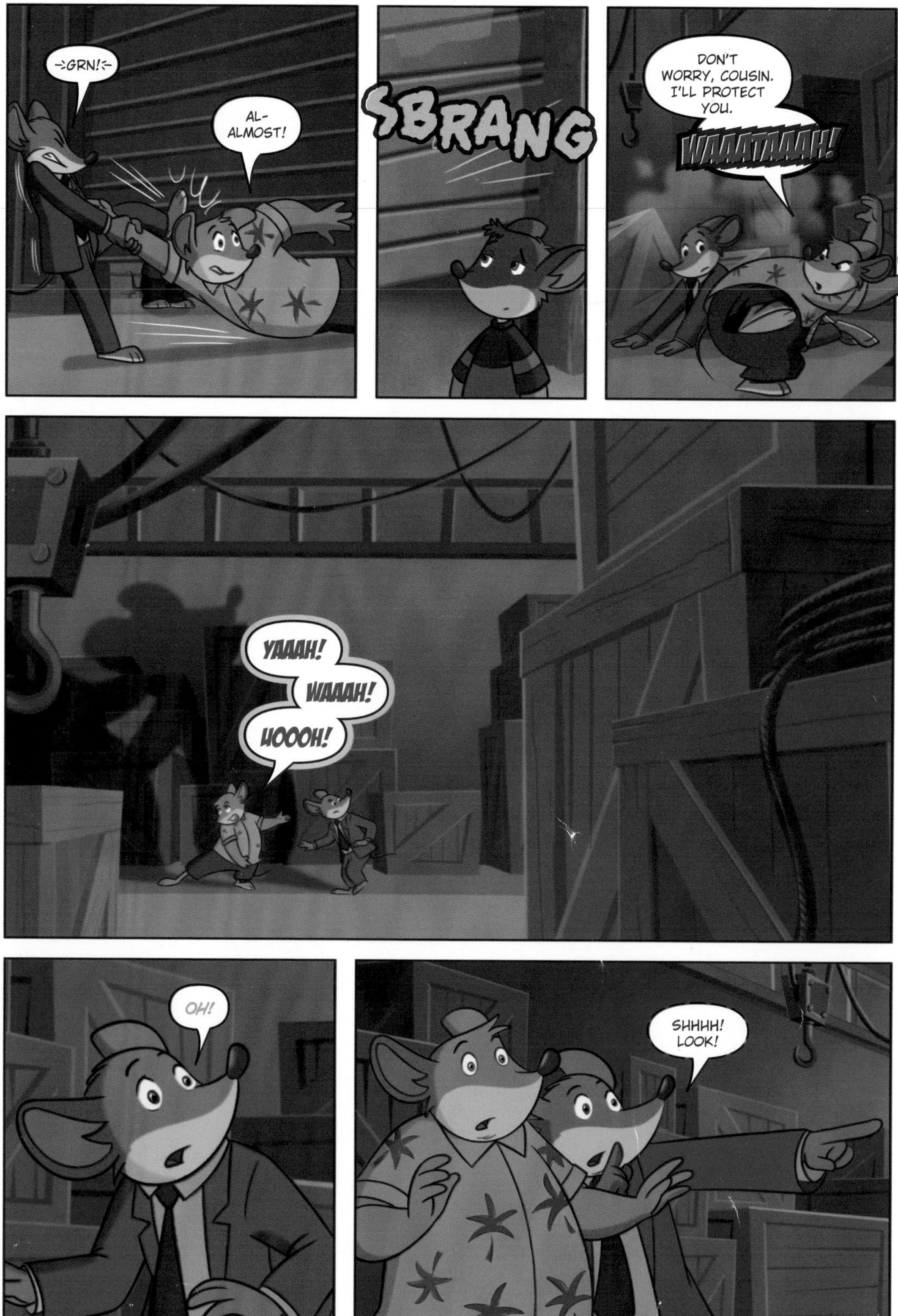

-GRN!-
AL-ALMOST!
SBRANG
DON'T WORRY, COUSIN. I'LL PROTECT YOU.
WAAATAAAH!
YAAAH!
WAAAH!
UOOOH!
OH!
SHHHH! LOOK!

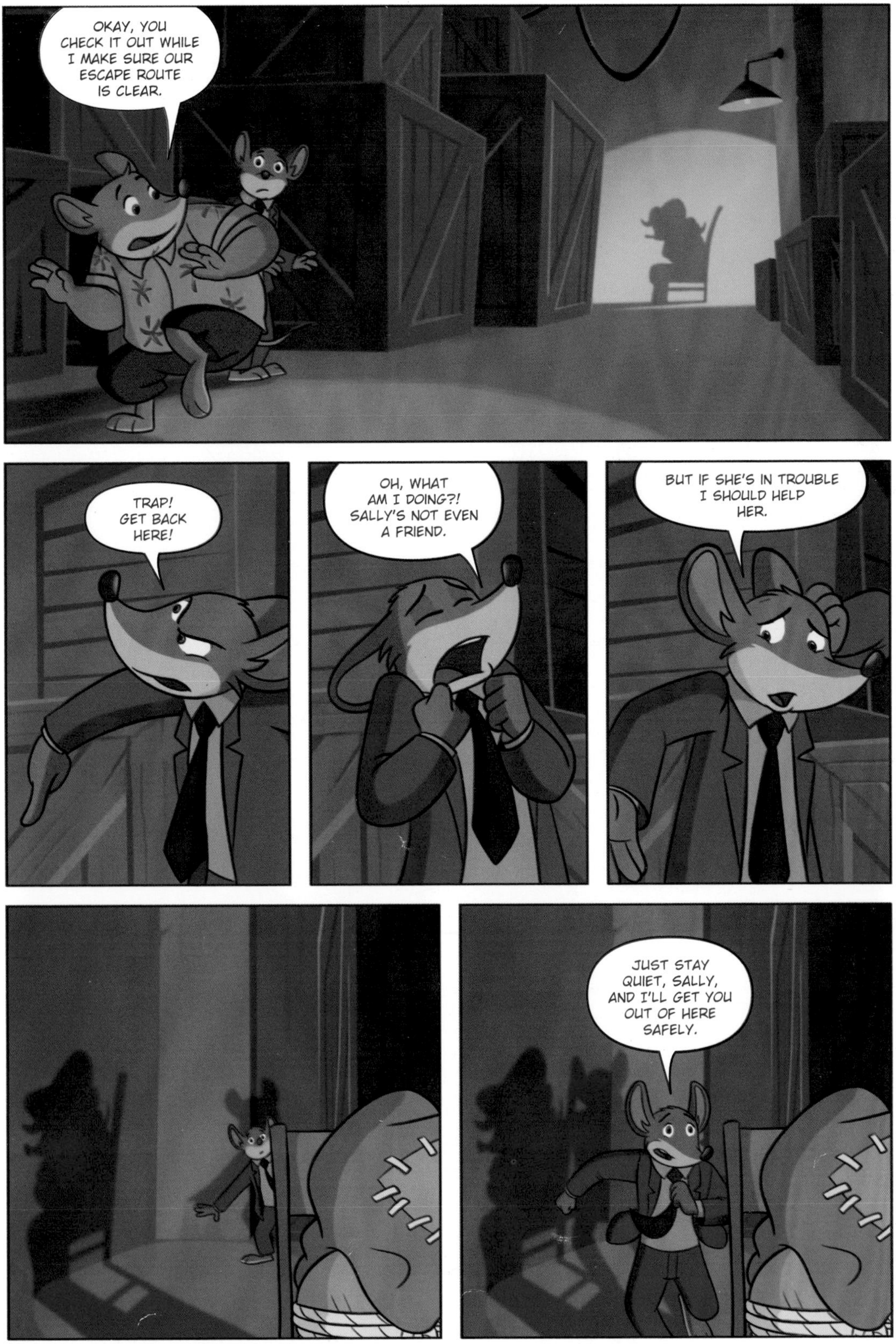

OKAY, YOU CHECK IT OUT WHILE I MAKE SURE OUR ESCAPE ROUTE IS CLEAR.
TRAP! GET BACK HERE!
OH, WHAT AM I DOING?! SALLY'S NOT EVEN A FRIEND.
BUT IF SHE'S IN TROUBLE I SHOULD HELP HER.
JUST STAY QUIET, SALLY, AND I'LL GET YOU OUT OF HERE SAFELY.

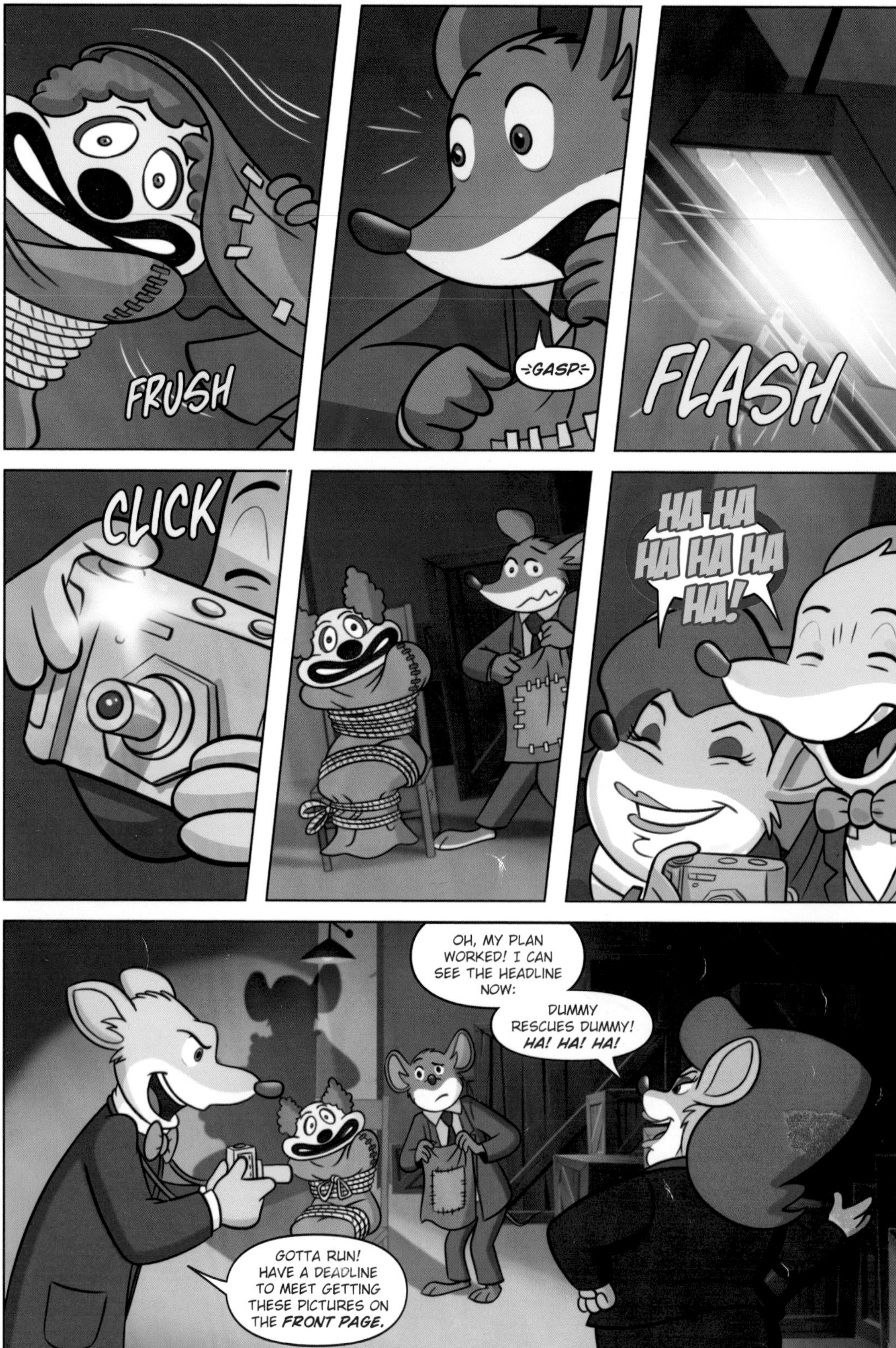

FRUSH
GASP
FLASH
CLICK
HA HA HA HA HA HA!
OH, MY PLAN WORKED! I CAN SEE THE HEADLINE NOW:
DUMMY RESCUES DUMMY! *HA! HA! HA!*
GOTTA RUN! HAVE A DEADLINE TO MEET GETTING THESE PICTURES ON THE *FRONT PAGE.*

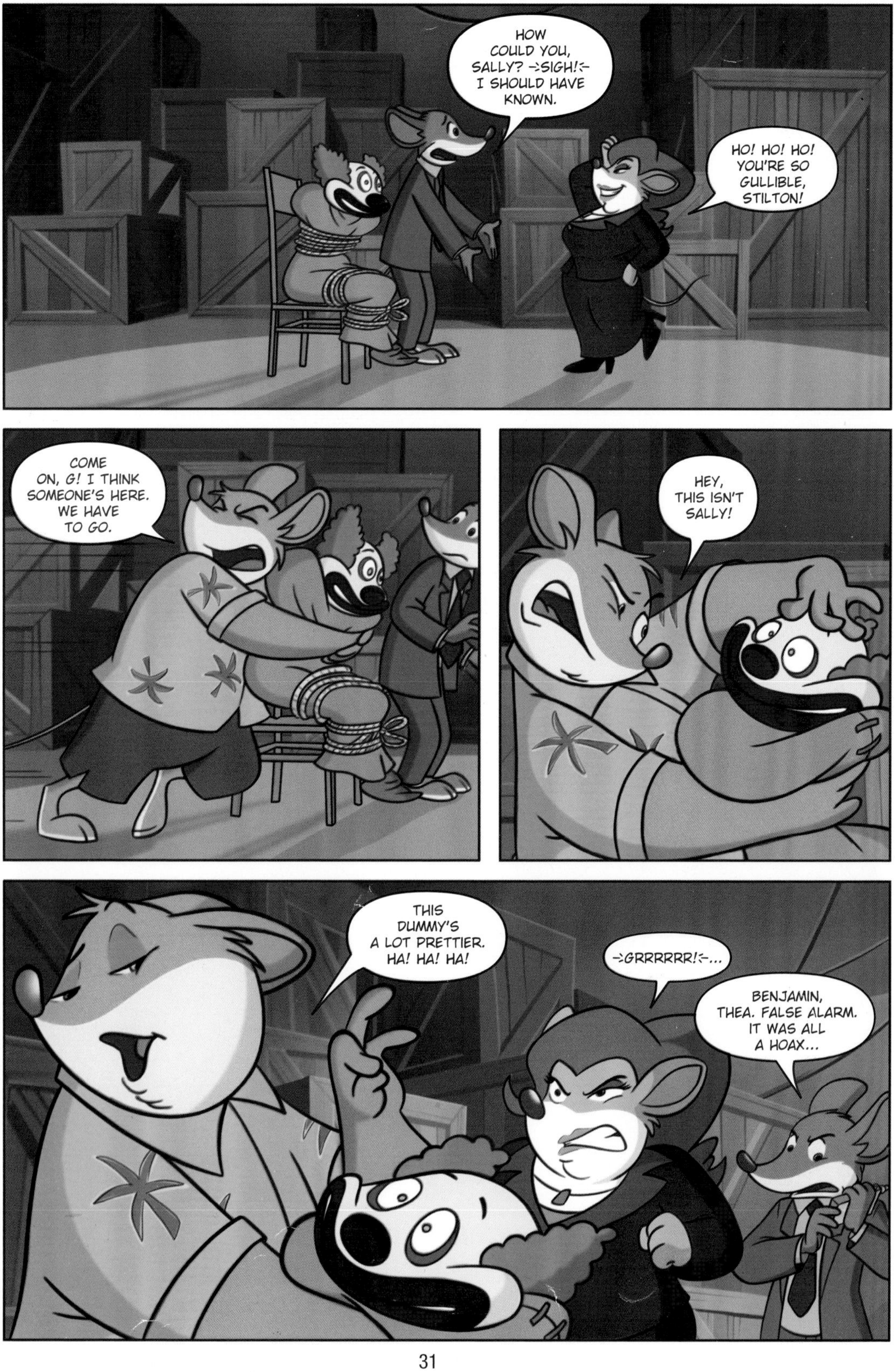
HOW COULD YOU, SALLY? ⇢SIGH!⇠ I SHOULD HAVE KNOWN.
HO! HO! HO! YOU'RE SO GULLIBLE, STILTON!
COME ON, G! I THINK SOMEONE'S HERE. WE HAVE TO GO.
HEY, THIS ISN'T SALLY!
THIS DUMMY'S A LOT PRETTIER. HA! HA! HA!
⇢GRRRRRR!⇠...
BENJAMIN, THEA. FALSE ALARM. IT WAS ALL A HOAX...

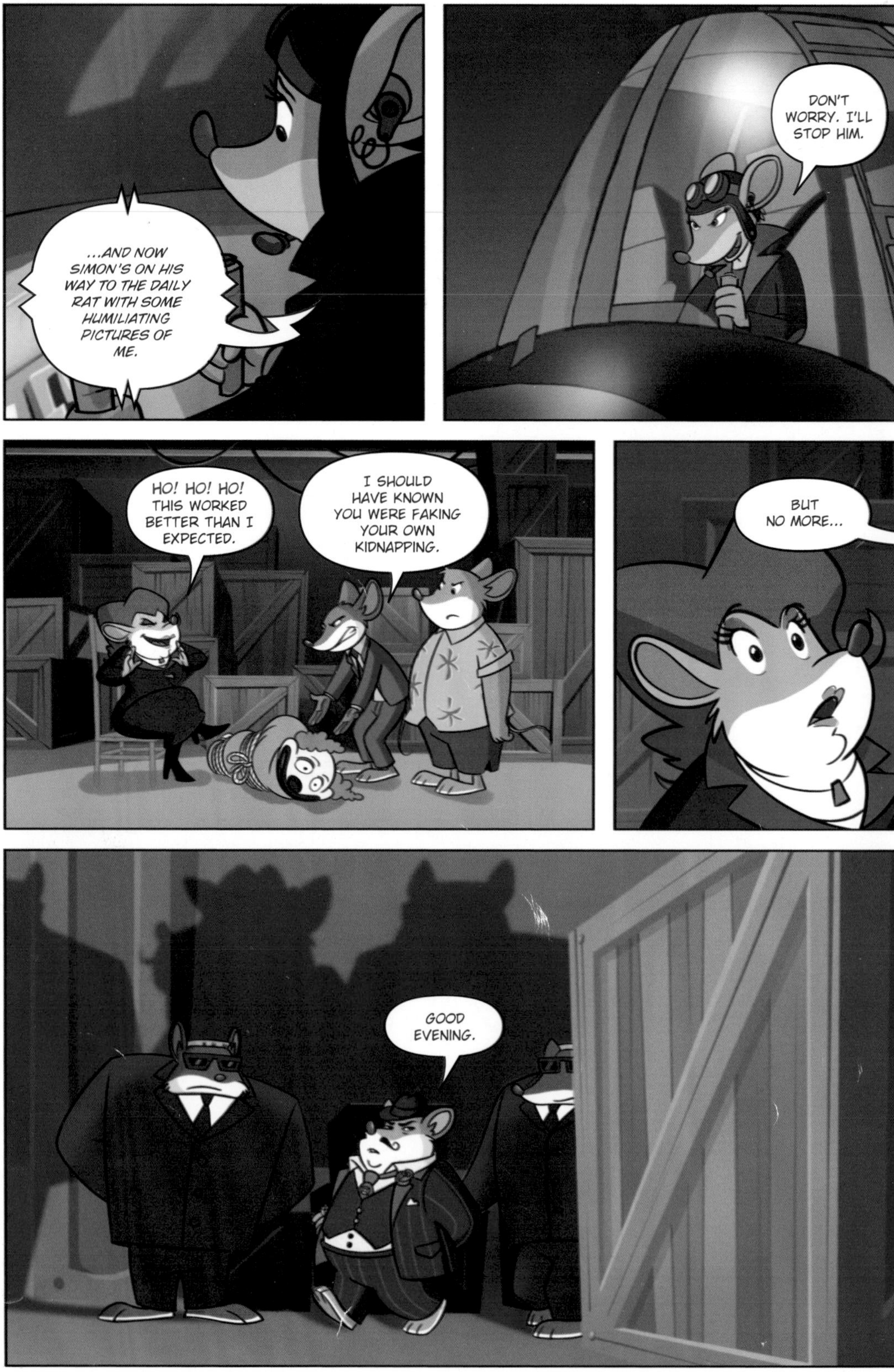
...AND NOW SIMON'S ON HIS WAY TO THE DAILY RAT WITH SOME HUMILIATING PICTURES OF ME.
DON'T WORRY. I'LL STOP HIM.
HO! HO! HO! THIS WORKED BETTER THAN I EXPECTED.
I SHOULD HAVE KNOWN YOU WERE FAKING YOUR OWN KIDNAPPING.
BUT NO MORE...
GOOD EVENING.

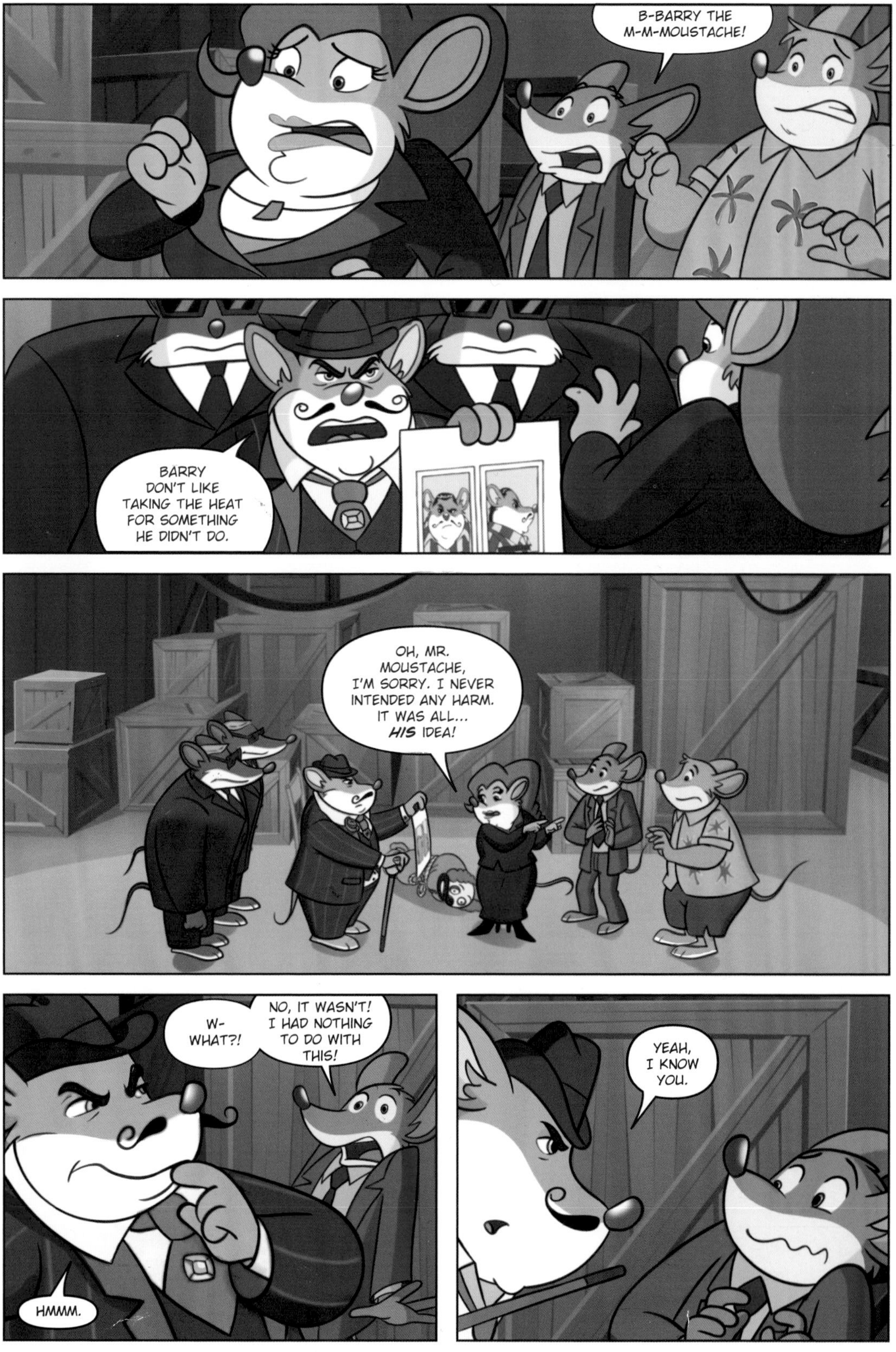
B-BARRY THE M-M-MOUSTACHE!
BARRY DON'T LIKE TAKING THE HEAT FOR SOMETHING HE DIDN'T DO.
OH, MR. MOUSTACHE, I'M SORRY. I NEVER INTENDED ANY HARM. IT WAS ALL... HIS IDEA!
W-WHAT?!
NO, IT WASN'T! I HAD NOTHING TO DO WITH THIS!
HMMM.
YEAH, I KNOW YOU.

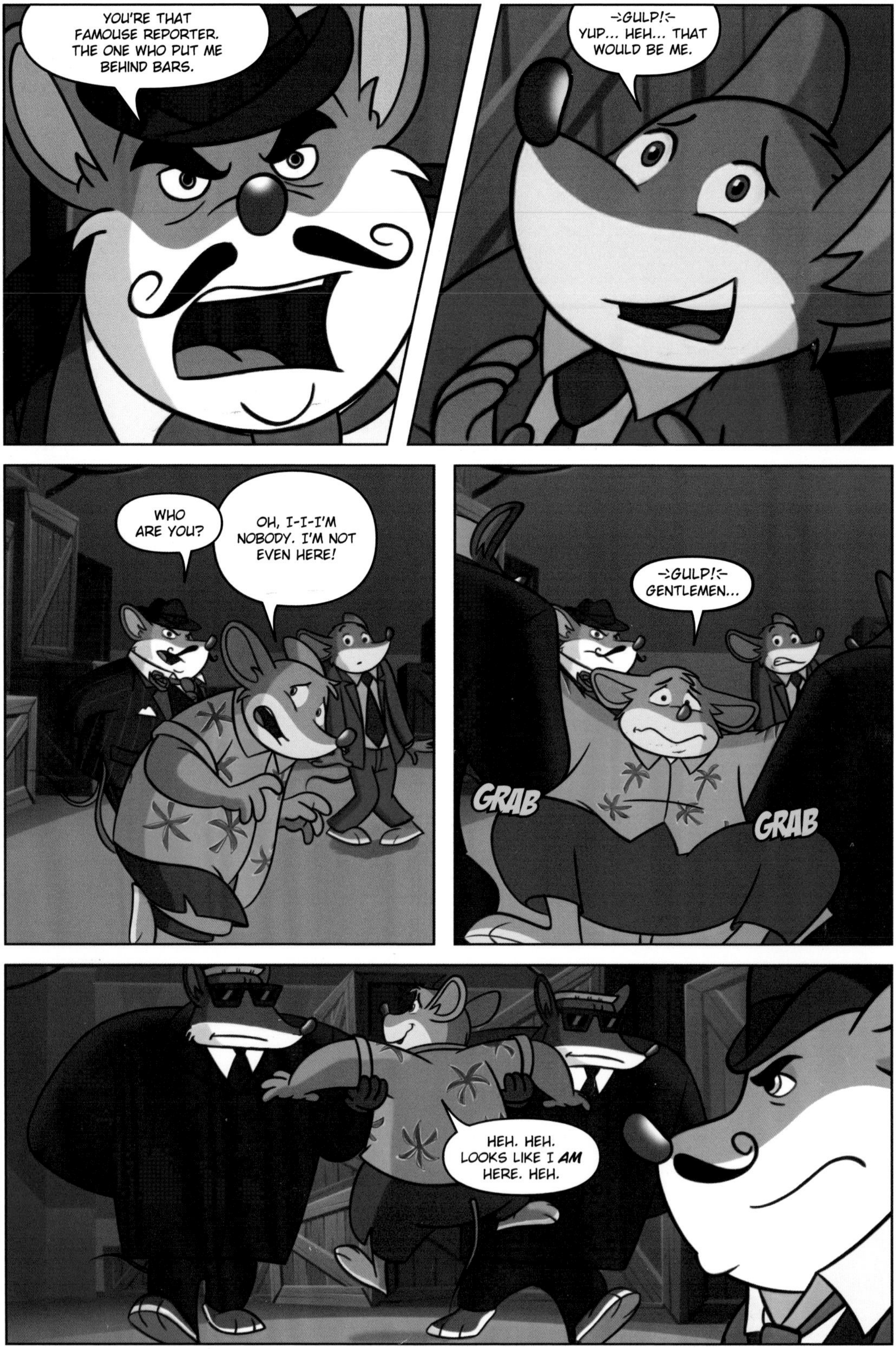
YOU'RE THAT FAMOUSE REPORTER. THE ONE WHO PUT ME BEHIND BARS.
-GULP!- YUP... HEH... THAT WOULD BE ME.
WHO ARE YOU?
OH, I-I-I'M NOBODY. I'M NOT EVEN HERE!
-GULP!- GENTLEMEN...
GRAB
GRAB
HEH. HEH. LOOKS LIKE I **AM** HERE. HEH.

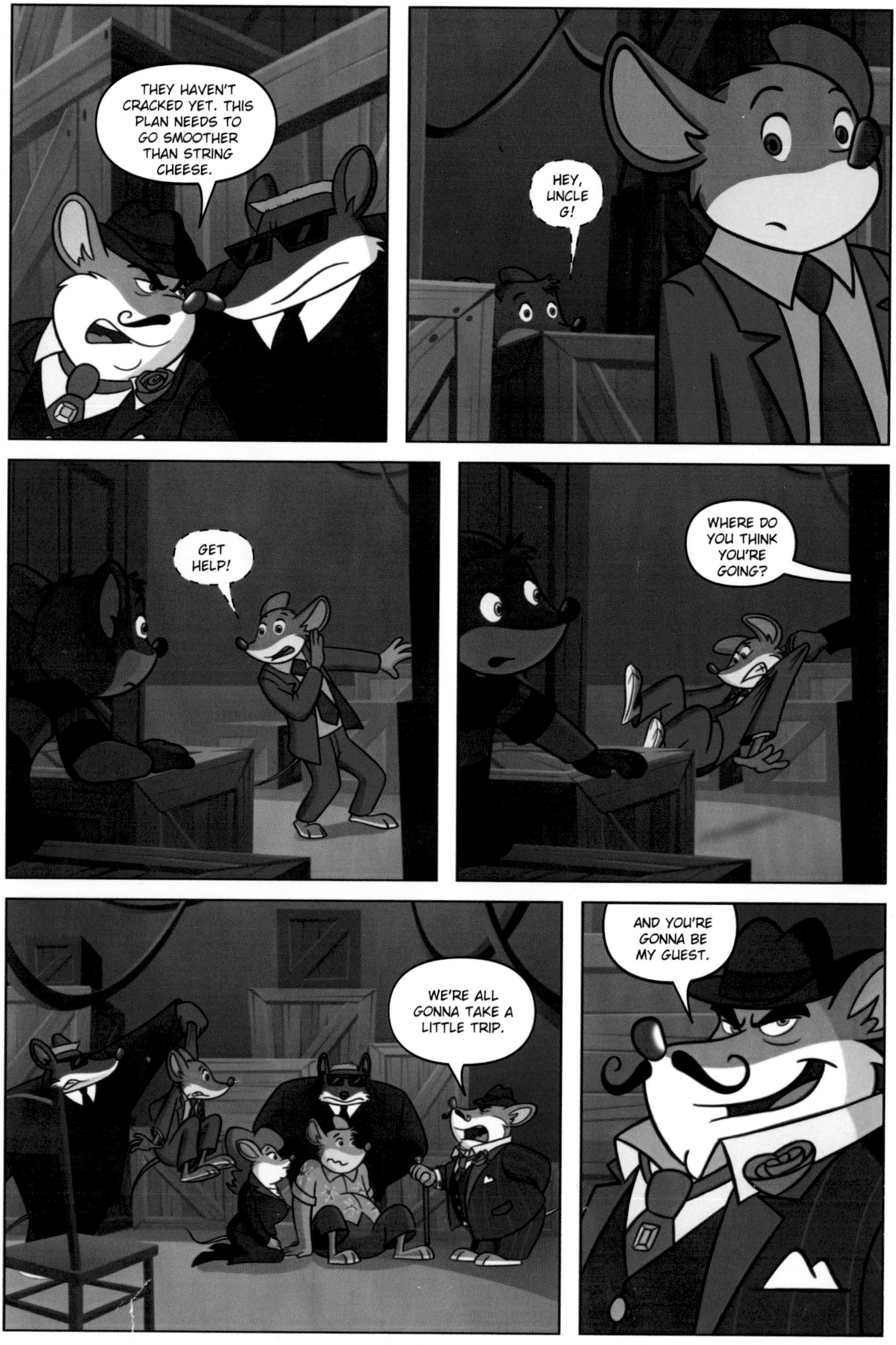
THEY HAVEN'T CRACKED YET. THIS PLAN NEEDS TO GO SMOOTHER THAN STRING CHEESE.
HEY, UNCLE G!
GET HELP!
WHERE DO YOU THINK YOU'RE GOING?
WE'RE ALL GONNA TAKE A LITTLE TRIP.
AND YOU'RE GONNA BE MY GUEST.

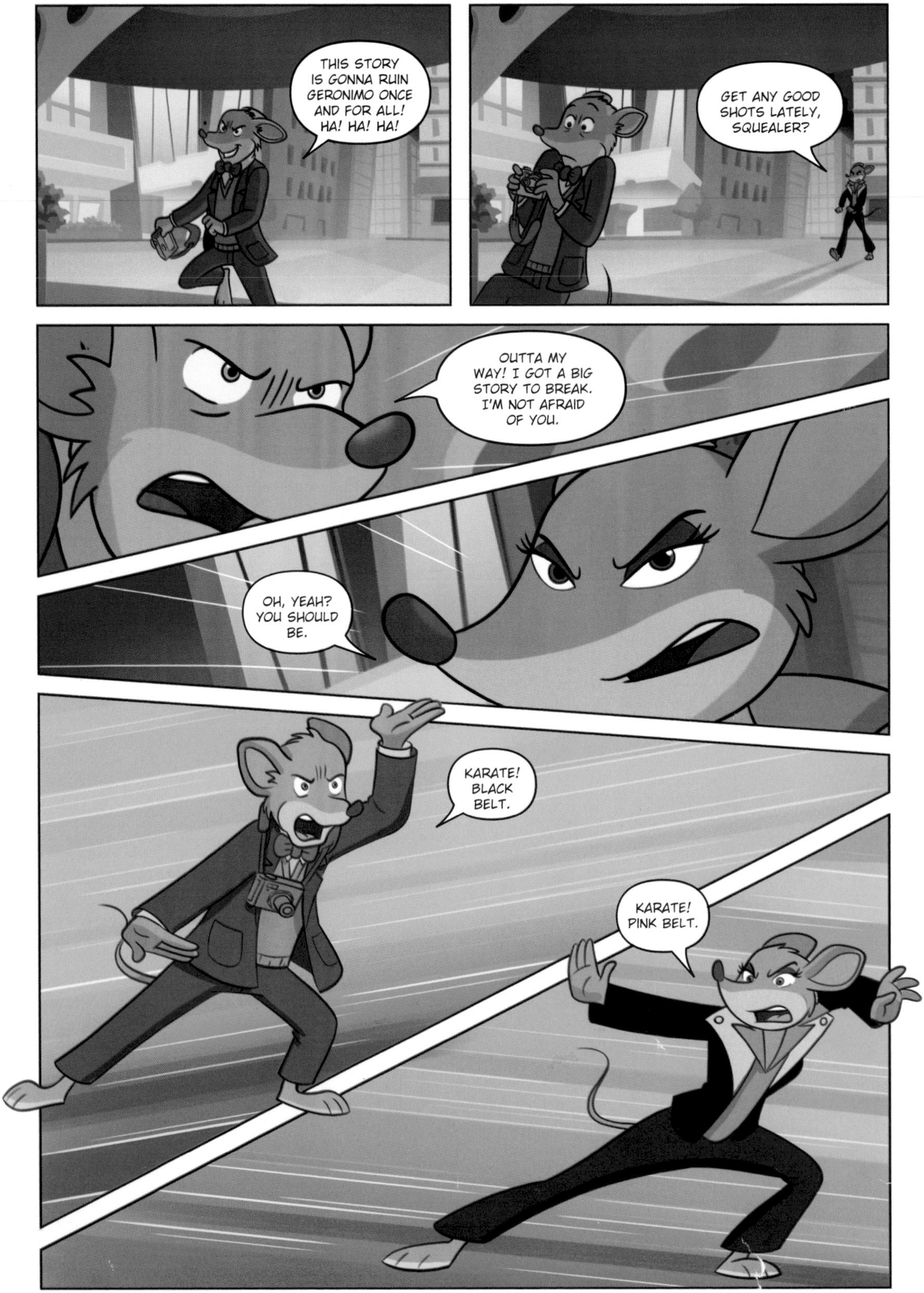
THIS STORY IS GONNA RUIN GERONIMO ONCE AND FOR ALL! HA! HA! HA!
GET ANY GOOD SHOTS LATELY, SQUEALER?
OUTTA MY WAY! I GOT A BIG STORY TO BREAK. I'M NOT AFRAID OF YOU.
OH, YEAH? YOU SHOULD BE.
KARATE! BLACK BELT.
KARATE! PINK BELT.

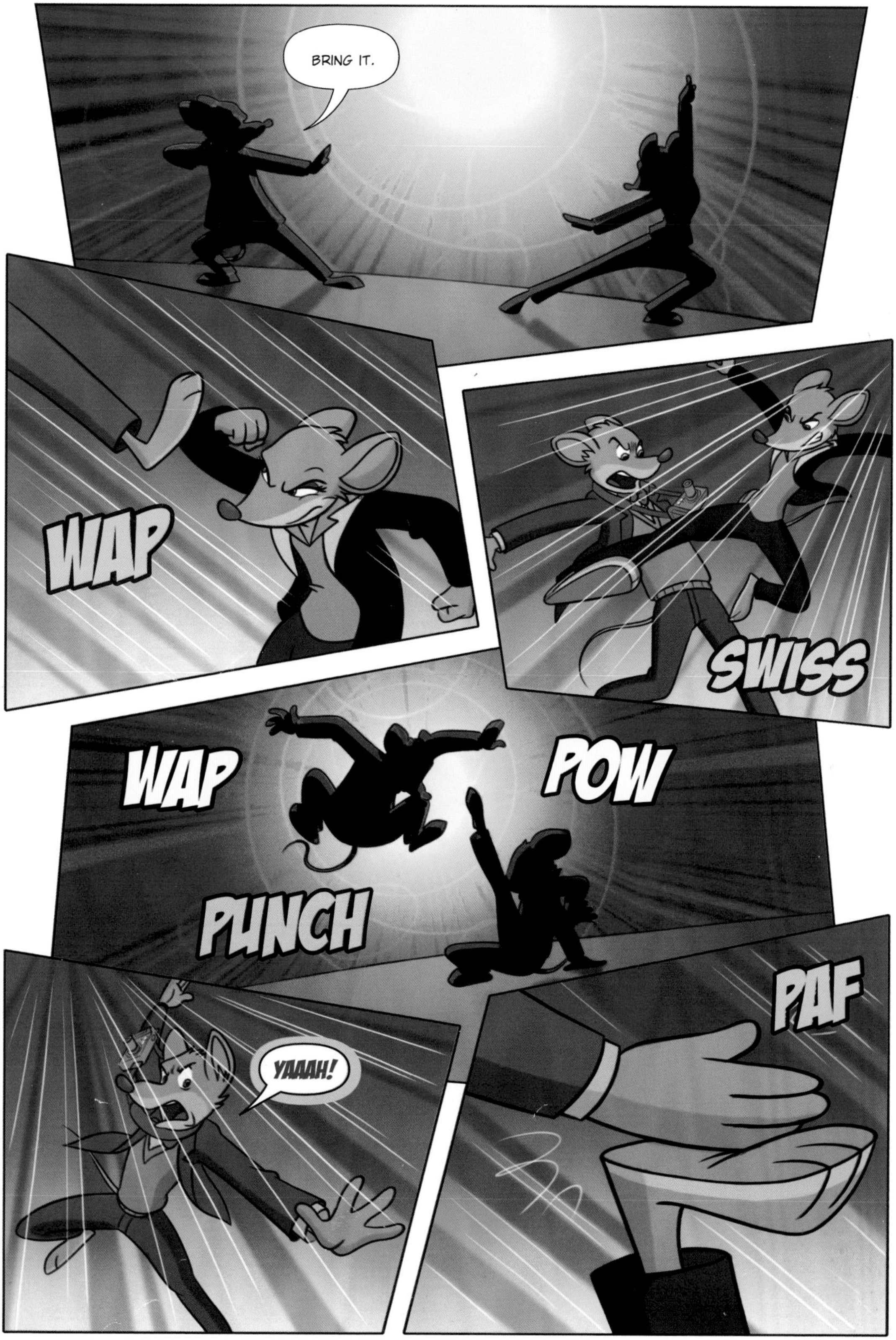
BRING IT.
WAP
SWISS
WAP
POW
PUNCH
YAAAH!
PAF

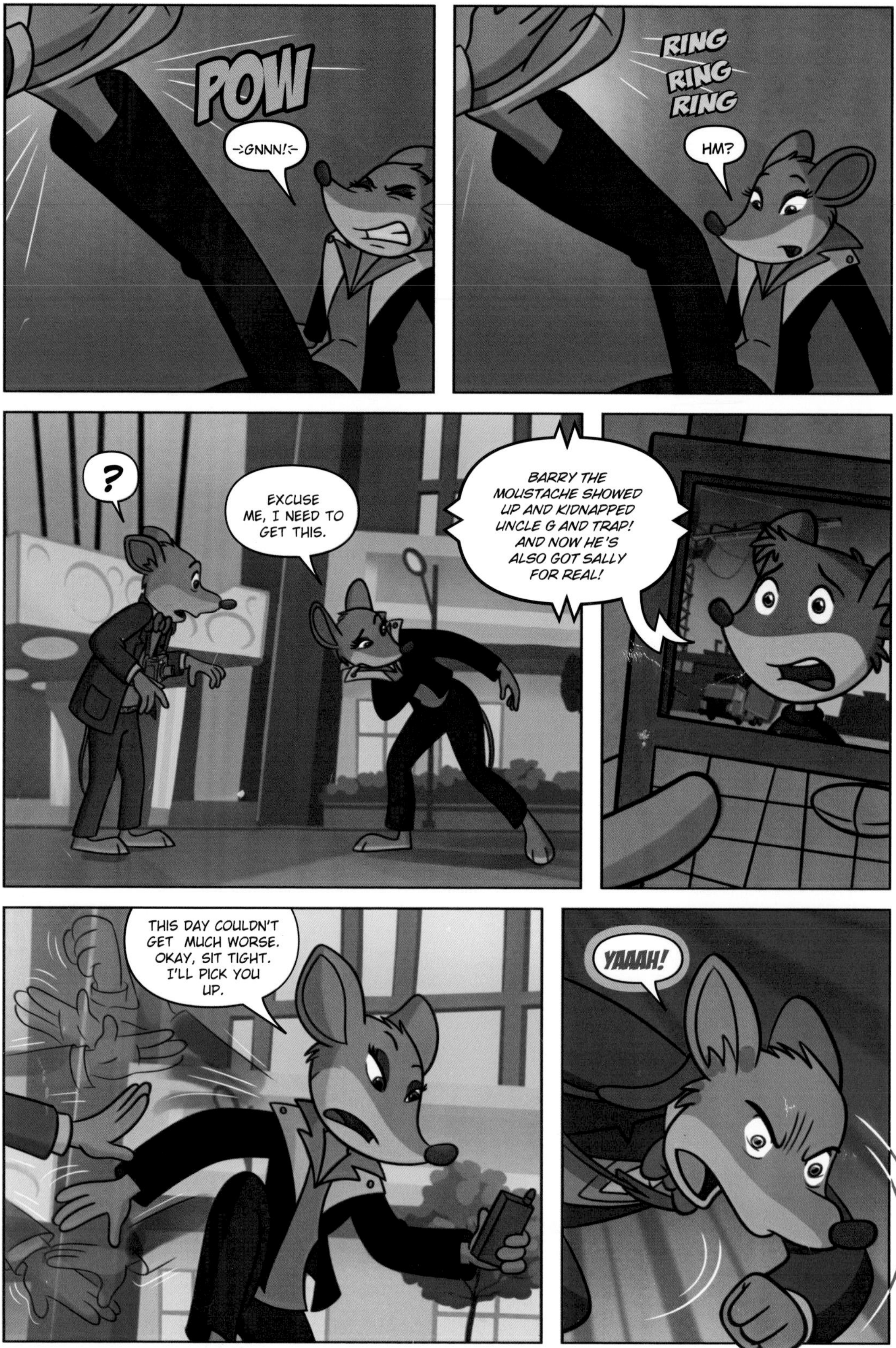
POW
GNNN!
RING
RING
RING
HM?
?
EXCUSE ME, I NEED TO GET THIS.
BARRY THE MOUSTACHE SHOWED UP AND KIDNAPPED UNCLE G AND TRAP! AND NOW HE'S ALSO GOT SALLY FOR REAL!
THIS DAY COULDN'T GET MUCH WORSE. OKAY, SIT TIGHT. I'LL PICK YOU UP.
YAAAH!

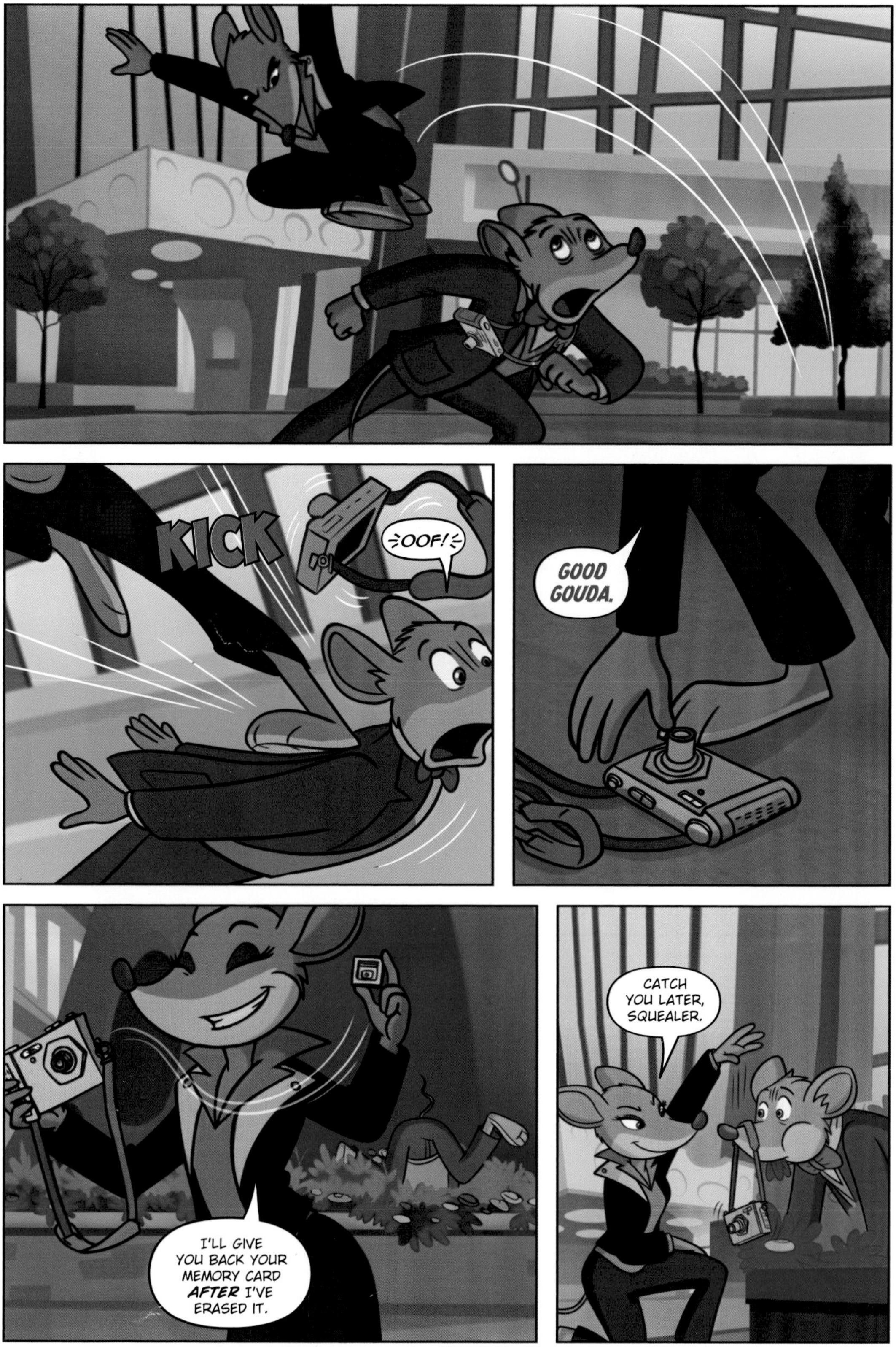
KICK
OOF!
GOOD GOUDA.
I'LL GIVE YOU BACK YOUR MEMORY CARD AFTER I'VE ERASED IT.
CATCH YOU LATER, SQUEALER.

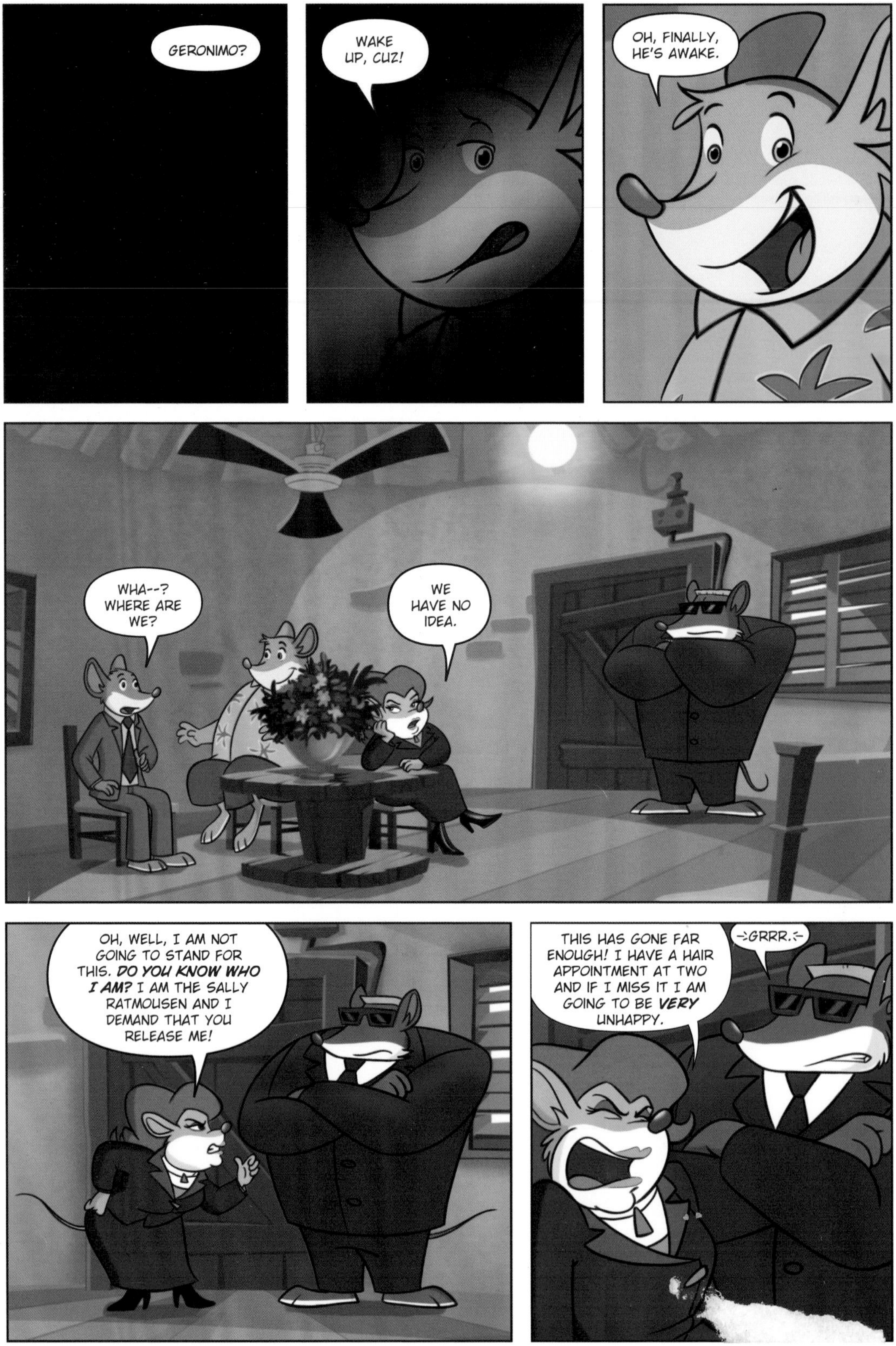
GERONIMO?
WAKE UP, CUZ!
OH, FINALLY, HE'S AWAKE.
WHA--? WHERE ARE WE?
WE HAVE NO IDEA.
OH, WELL, I AM NOT GOING TO STAND FOR THIS. ***DO YOU KNOW WHO I AM?*** I AM THE SALLY RATMOUSEN AND I DEMAND THAT YOU RELEASE ME!
THIS HAS GONE FAR ENOUGH! I HAVE A HAIR APPOINTMENT AT TWO AND IF I MISS IT I AM GOING TO BE ***VERY*** UNHAPPY.
GRRR.

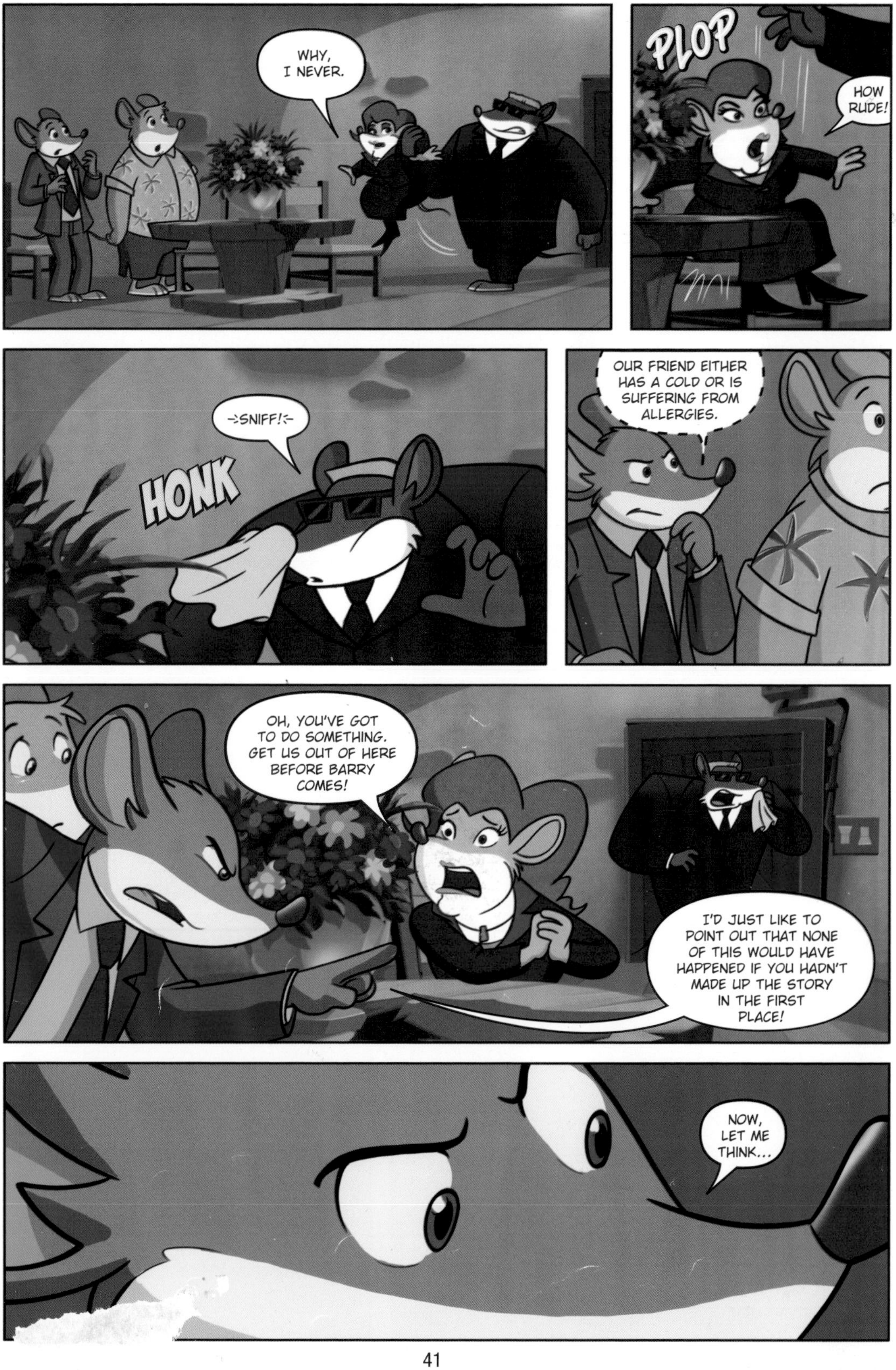
WHY, I NEVER.
PLOP
HOW RUDE!
SNIFF!
HONK
OUR FRIEND EITHER HAS A COLD OR IS SUFFERING FROM ALLERGIES.
OH, YOU'VE GOT TO DO SOMETHING. GET US OUT OF HERE BEFORE BARRY COMES!
I'D JUST LIKE TO POINT OUT THAT NONE OF THIS WOULD HAVE HAPPENED IF YOU HADN'T MADE UP THE STORY IN THE FIRST PLACE!
NOW, LET ME THINK...

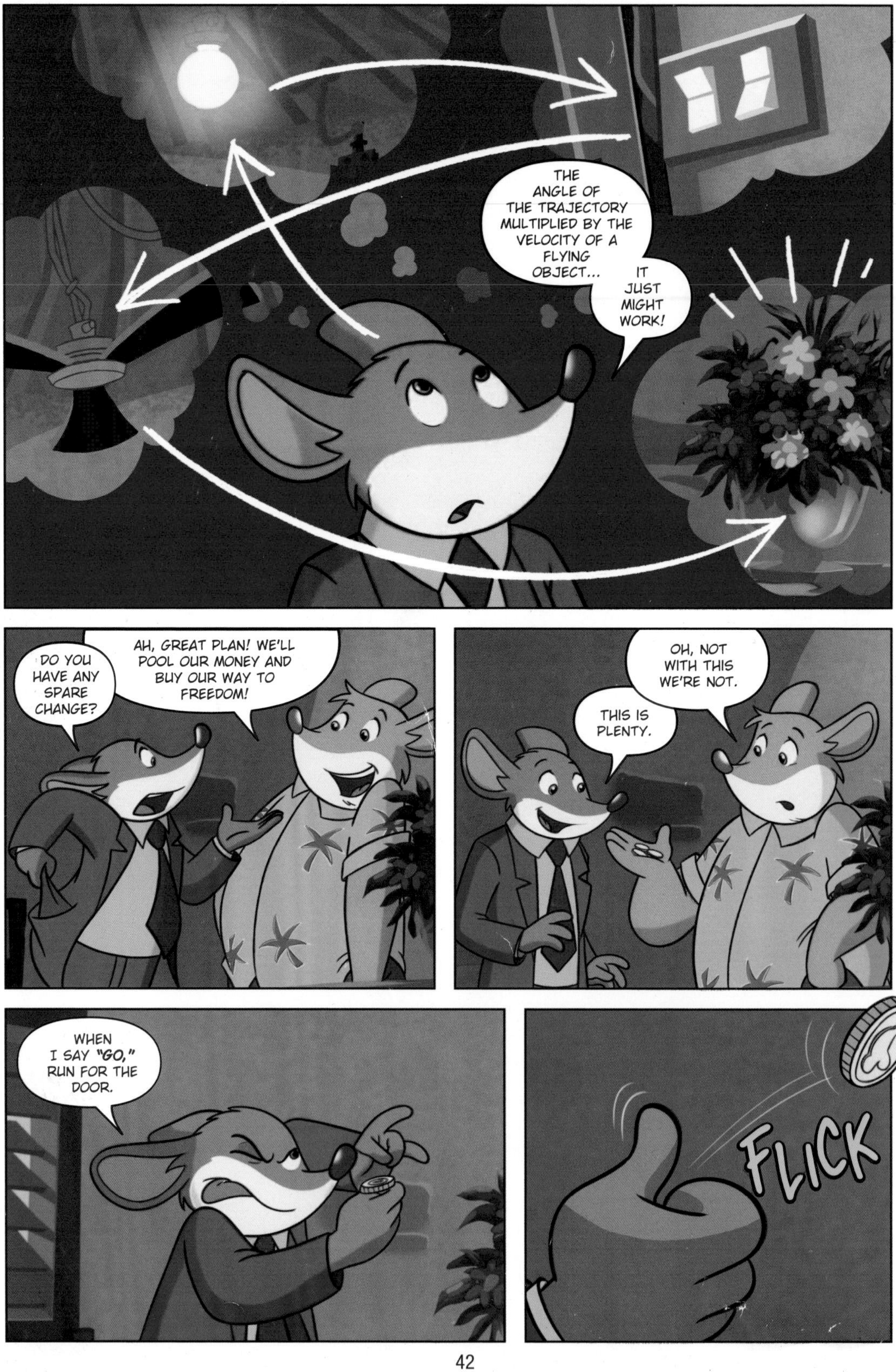
THE ANGLE OF THE TRAJECTORY MULTIPLIED BY THE VELOCITY OF A FLYING OBJECT...
IT JUST MIGHT WORK!
DO YOU HAVE ANY SPARE CHANGE?
AH, GREAT PLAN! WE'LL POOL OUR MONEY AND BUY OUR WAY TO FREEDOM!
OH, NOT WITH THIS WE'RE NOT.
THIS IS PLENTY.
WHEN I SAY "GO," RUN FOR THE DOOR.
FLICK

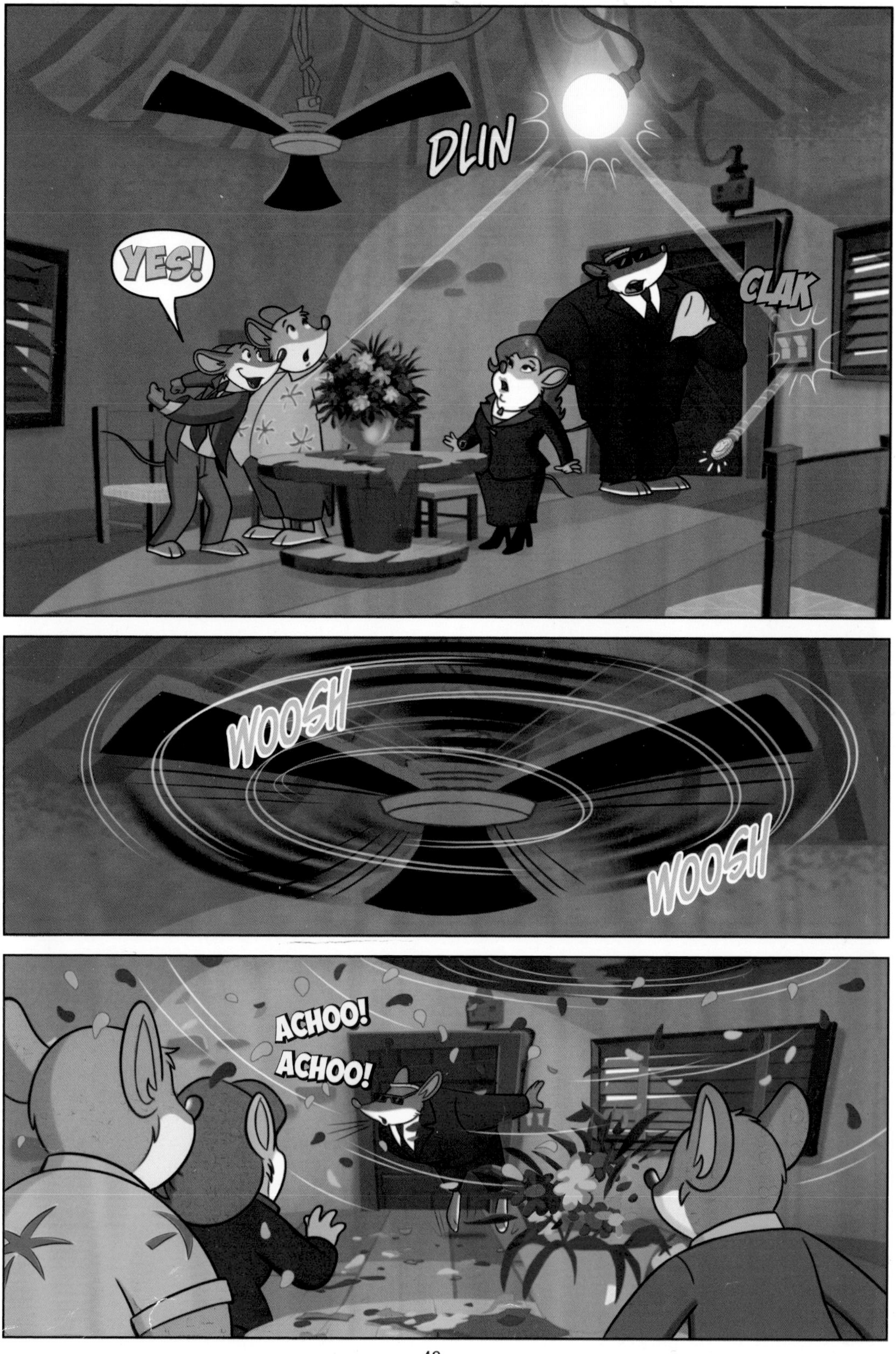
DLIN
YES!
CLAK
WOOSH
WOOSH
ACHOO!
ACHOO!

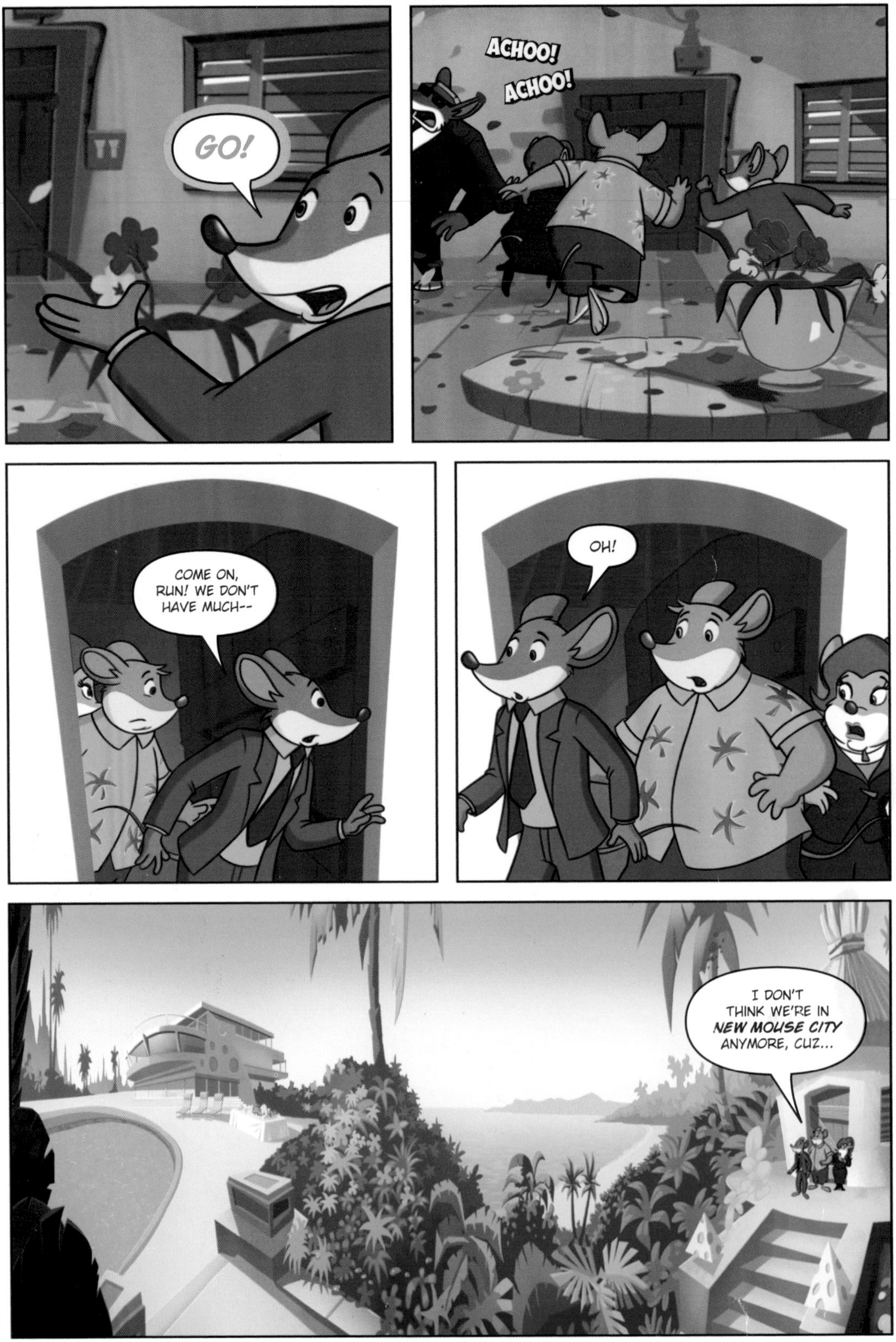
GO!
ACHOO!
ACHOO!
COME ON, RUN! WE DON'T HAVE MUCH--
OH!
I DON'T THINK WE'RE IN NEW MOUSE CITY ANYMORE, CUZ...

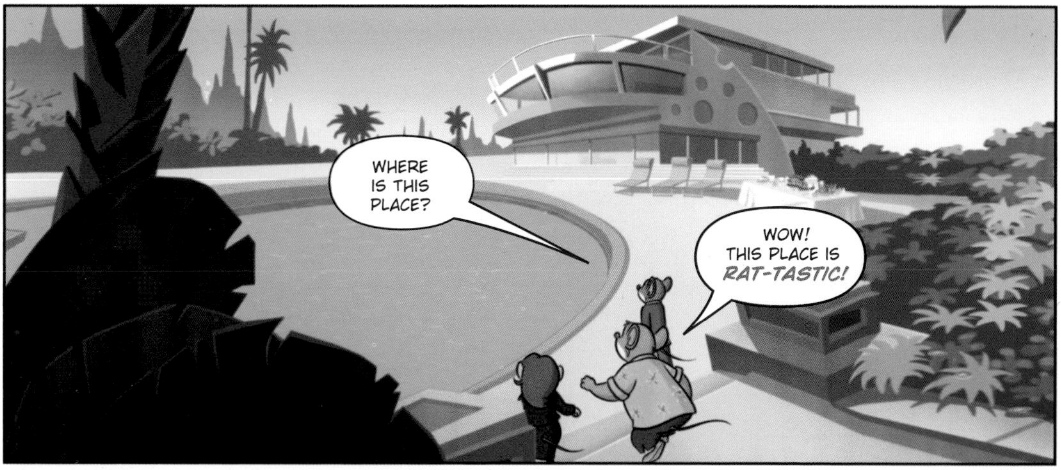
WHERE IS THIS PLACE?
WOW! THIS PLACE IS RAT-TASTIC!

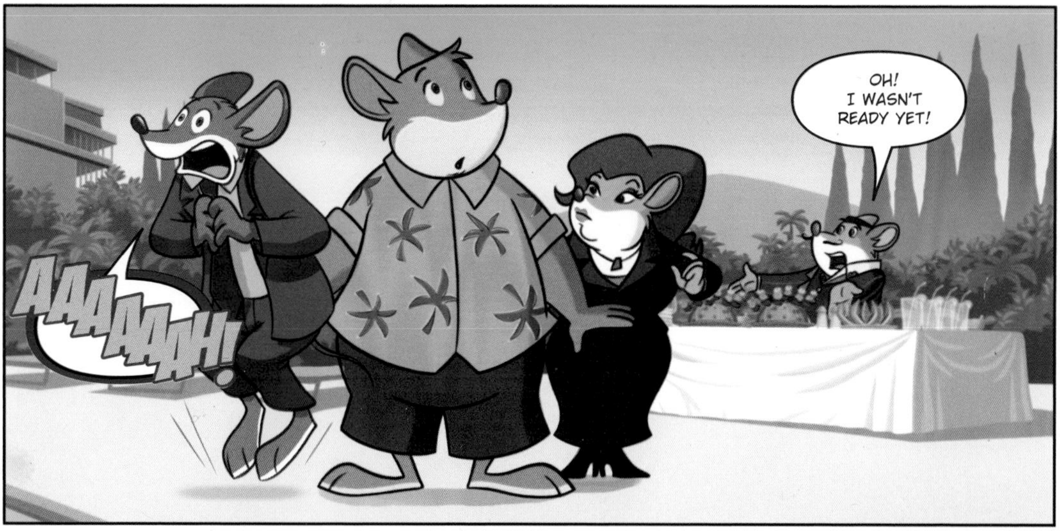
AAAAAAAH!
OH! I WASN'T READY YET!

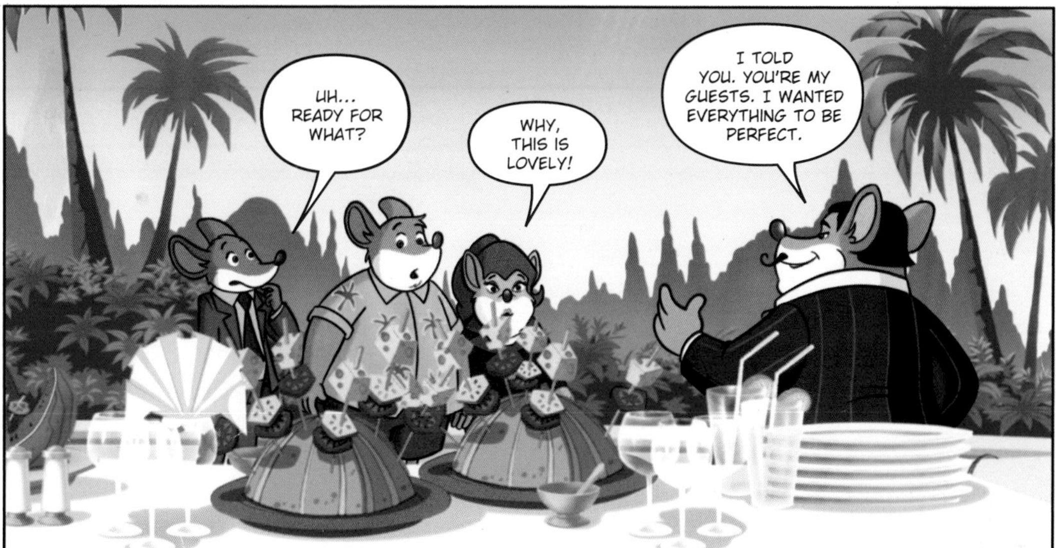
UH... READY FOR WHAT?
WHY, THIS IS LOVELY!
I TOLD YOU. YOU'RE MY GUESTS. I WANTED EVERYTHING TO BE PERFECT.

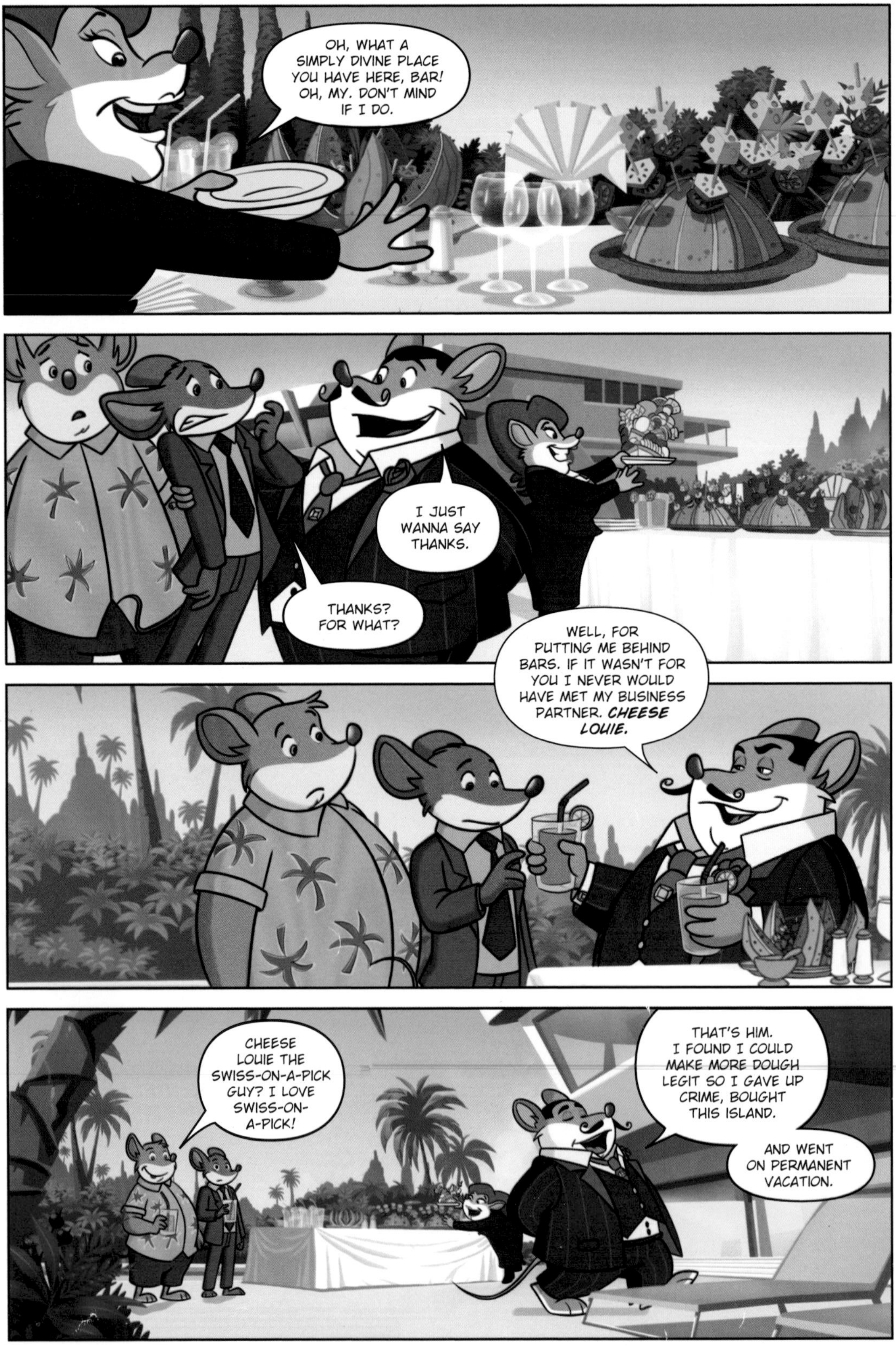
OH, WHAT A SIMPLY DIVINE PLACE YOU HAVE HERE, BAR! OH, MY. DON'T MIND IF I DO.
I JUST WANNA SAY THANKS.
THANKS? FOR WHAT?
WELL, FOR PUTTING ME BEHIND BARS. IF IT WASN'T FOR YOU I NEVER WOULD HAVE MET MY BUSINESS PARTNER. CHEESE LOUIE.
CHEESE LOUIE THE SWISS-ON-A-PICK GUY? I LOVE SWISS-ON-A-PICK!
THAT'S HIM. I FOUND I COULD MAKE MORE DOUGH LEGIT SO I GAVE UP CRIME, BOUGHT THIS ISLAND.
AND WENT ON PERMANENT VACATION.

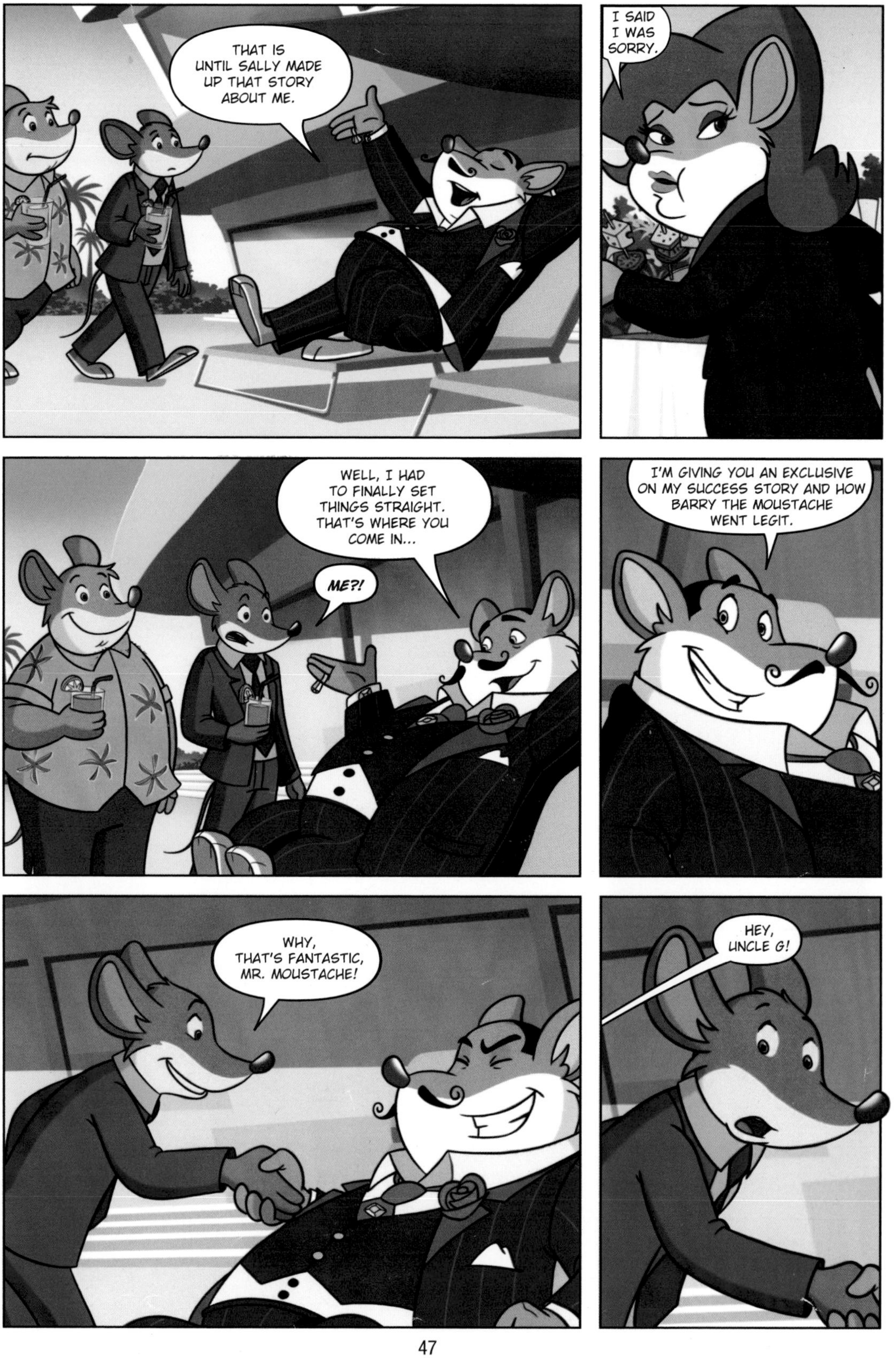
THAT IS UNTIL SALLY MADE UP THAT STORY ABOUT ME.
I SAID I WAS SORRY.
WELL, I HAD TO FINALLY SET THINGS STRAIGHT. THAT'S WHERE YOU COME IN...
ME?!
I'M GIVING YOU AN EXCLUSIVE ON MY SUCCESS STORY AND HOW BARRY THE MOUSTACHE WENT LEGIT.
WHY, THAT'S FANTASTIC, MR. MOUSTACHE!
HEY, UNCLE G!

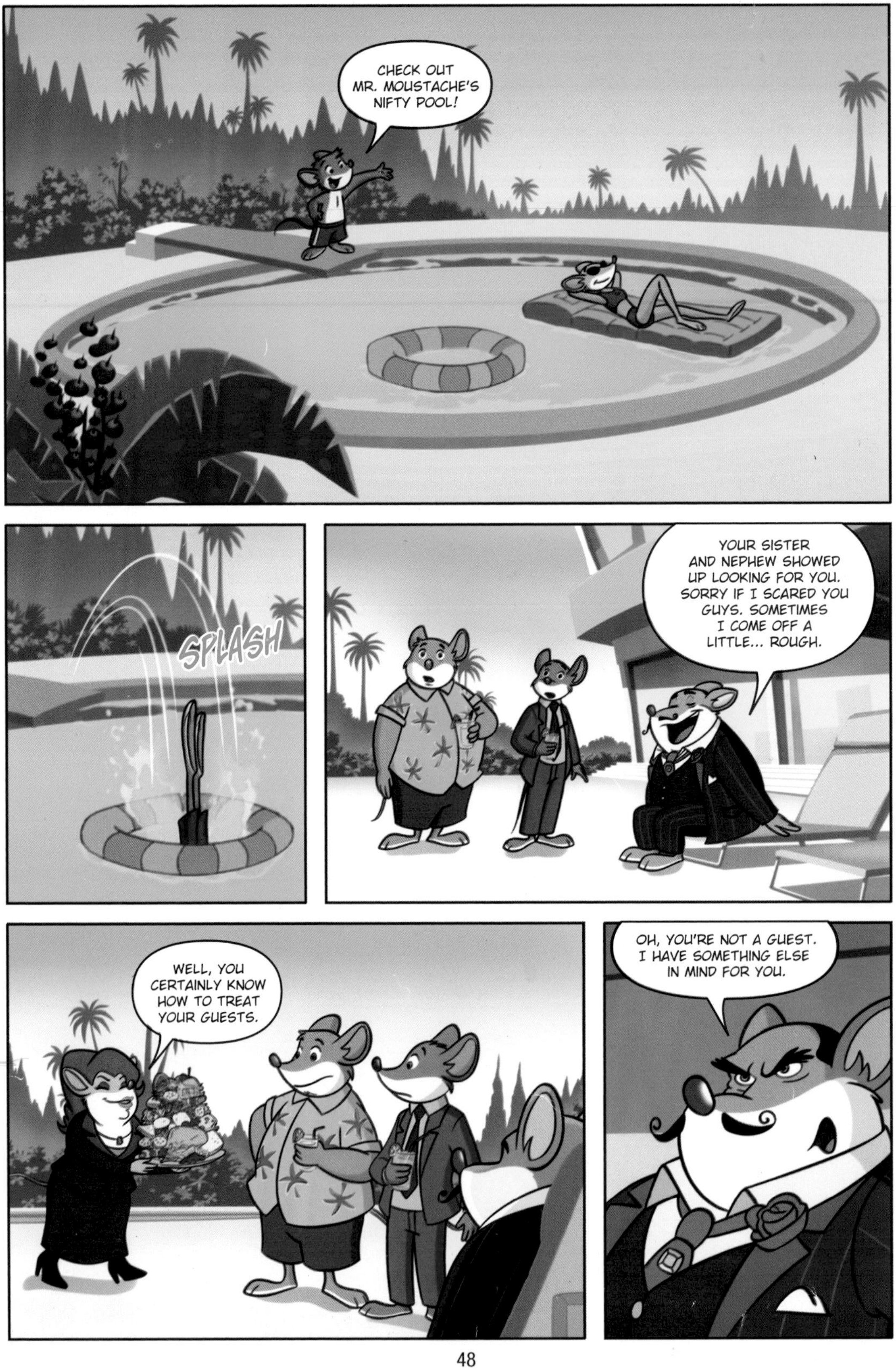
CHECK OUT MR. MOUSTACHE'S NIFTY POOL!
SPLASH
YOUR SISTER AND NEPHEW SHOWED UP LOOKING FOR YOU. SORRY IF I SCARED YOU GUYS. SOMETIMES I COME OFF A LITTLE... ROUGH.
WELL, YOU CERTAINLY KNOW HOW TO TREAT YOUR GUESTS.
OH, YOU'RE NOT A GUEST. I HAVE SOMETHING ELSE IN MIND FOR YOU.

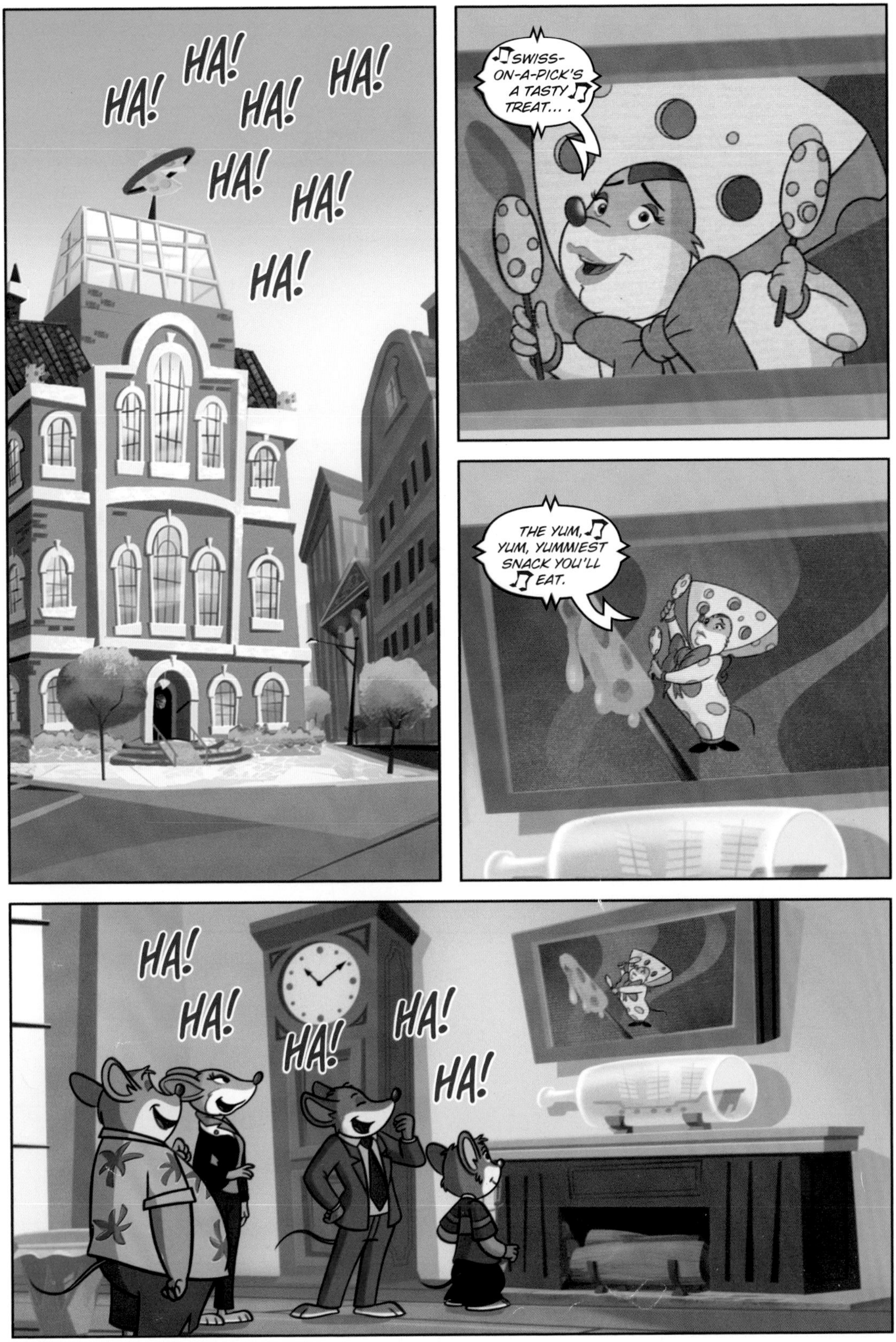
HA! HA! HA! HA! HA! HA! HA!
♫SWISS-ON-A-PICK'S A TASTY ♫ TREAT. . . .
THE YUM, ♫ YUM, YUMMIEST SNACK YOU'LL ♫ EAT.
HA! HA! HA! HA! HA!

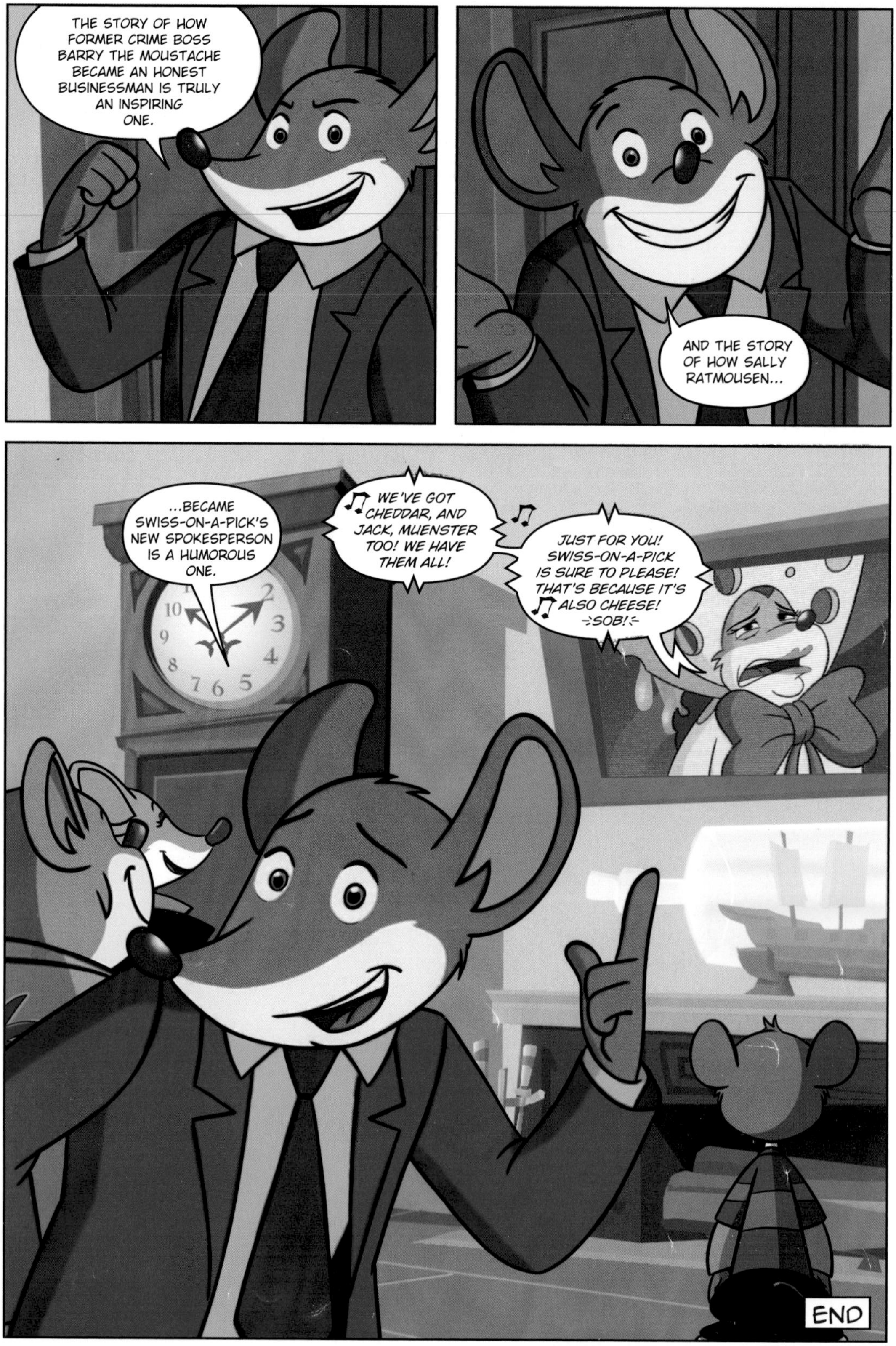
THE STORY OF HOW FORMER CRIME BOSS BARRY THE MOUSTACHE BECAME AN HONEST BUSINESSMAN IS TRULY AN INSPIRING ONE.
AND THE STORY OF HOW SALLY RATMOUSEN...
...BECAME SWISS-ON-A-PICK'S NEW SPOKESPERSON IS A HUMOROUS ONE.
WE'VE GOT CHEDDAR, AND JACK, MUENSTER TOO! WE HAVE THEM ALL!
JUST FOR YOU! SWISS-ON-A-PICK IS SURE TO PLEASE! THAT'S BECAUSE IT'S ALSO CHEESE! -SOB!-
END

Watch Out For PAPERCUTZ ™

Welcome to the fast-paced, fun-filled, fifth GERONIMO STILTON graphic novel, "Barry the Moustache," the official comics adaptation of the fifth episode of Geronimo Stilton, Season One, written by Temple Mathews, brought to you by Papercutz—those ink-stained wretches dedicated to publishing great graphic novels for all ages. I'm Salicrup, *Jim Salicrup,* the Editor-in-Chief and professional Papa Smurf lookalike, here with BREAKING NEWS! News that Geronimo himself wishes he had for *The Rodent's Gazette* and Simon Squealer and Sally Ratmousen wanted for *The Daily Rat*, but *The New York Times* scooped them all! Here's the story… Papercutz has managed to get the North American rights to publish perhaps the most successful comics series in the world—ASTERIX! Now some of you may not have heard of this Asterix fella, so let's take a quick journey in the Geronimo's old time machine, the Speedrat…

We're back in the year 50 BC in the ancient country of Gaul, located where France, Belgium, and the Southern Netherlands are today. All of Gaul has been conquered by the Romans… well, not all of it. One tiny village, inhabited by indomitable Gauls, resists the invaders again and again. That doesn't make it easy for the garrisons of Roman soldiers surrounding the village in fortified camps.

So, how's it possible that a small village can hold its own against the mighty Roman Empire? The answer is this guy…

This is **Asterix**. A shrewd, little warrior of keen intellect… and superhuman strength. Asterix gets his superhuman strength from a magic potion. But he's not alone.

Obelix is Asterix's inseparable friend. He too has superhuman strength. He's a menhir (tall, upright stone monuments) deliveryman, he loves eating wild boar and getting into brawls. Obelix is always ready to drop everything to go off on a new adventure with Asterix.

Panoramix, the village's venerable Druid, gathers mistletoe and prepares magic potions. His greatest success is the power potion. When a villager drinks this magical elixir he or she is temporarily granted super-strength. This is just one of the Druid's potions! And now you know why this small village can survive, despite seemingly impossible odds.

While we're here, we may as well meet a couple of other Gauls…

Cacofonix is the bard—the village poet. Opinions about his talents are divided: he thinks he's awesome, everybody else thinks he's awful, but when he doesn't sing anything, he's a cheerful companion and well-liked…

Vitalstatistix, finally, is the village's chief. Majestic, courageous, and irritable, the old warrior is respected by his men and feared by his enemies. Vitalstatistix has only one fear: that the sky will fall on his head but, as he says himself, "That'll be the day!"

There are plenty more characters around here, but you've met enough for now. It's time we get back to the palatial Papercutz offices and wrap this up. Now, where did we park the Speedrat…? Oh, there it is!

And we're back! We'll return to The Philosophy of Geronimo Stilton in the *Watch Out for Papercutz* page in GERONIMO STILTON REPORTER #6 "Paws Off, Cheddarface!" Check out the preview of that thrilling Geronimo adventure on the following pages – and look for ASTERIX and GERONIMO STILTON REPORTER at your favorite library or bookseller. You'll be glad you did!

Jim

STAY IN TOUCH!

EMAIL: salicrup@papercutz.com
WEB: papercutz.com
TWITTER: @papercutzgn
INSTAGRAM: @papercutzgn
FACEBOOK: PAPERCUTZGRAPHICNOVELS
SNAIL MAIL: Papercutz, 160 Broadway, Suite 700, East Wing, New York, NY 10038

Special Preview of GERONIMO STILTON REPORTER Graphic Novel #6
"Paws Off, Cheddarface!"

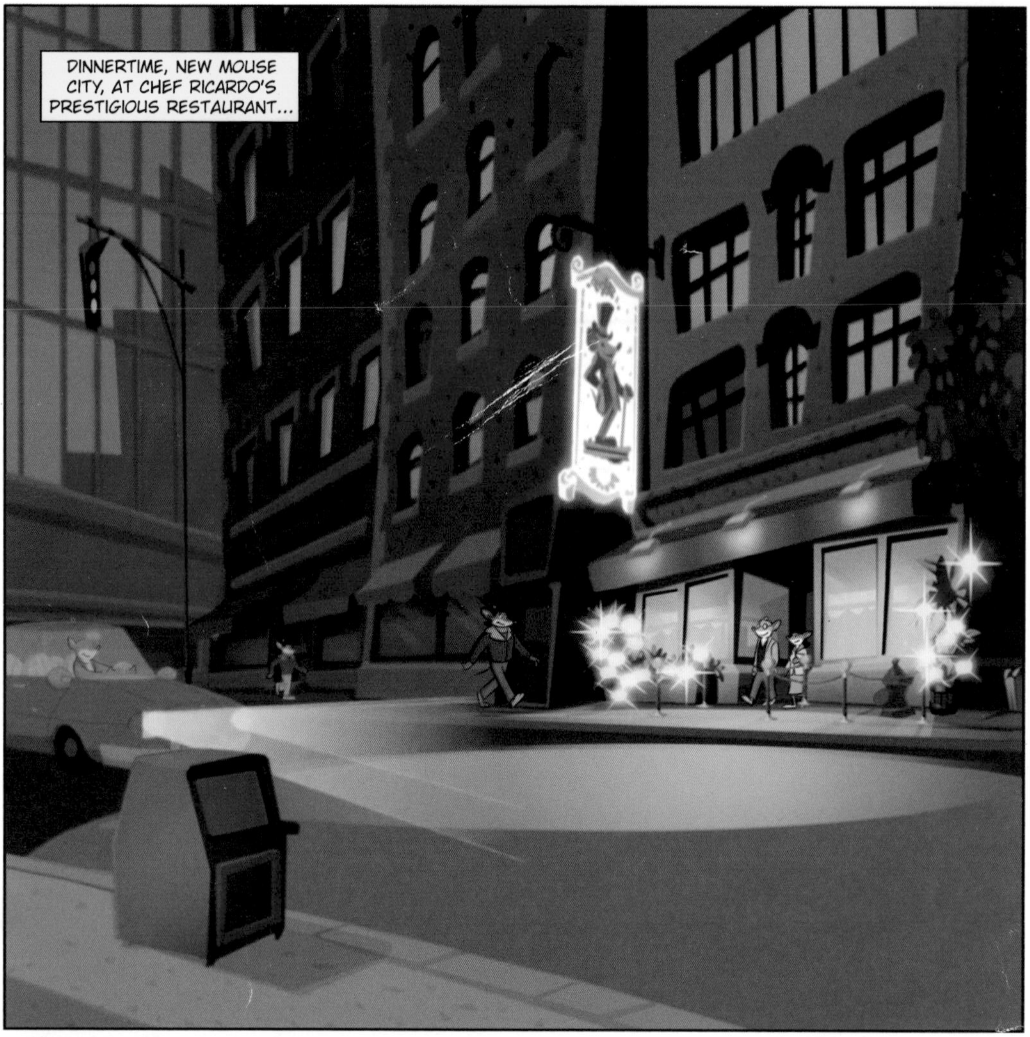
DINNERTIME, NEW MOUSE CITY, AT CHEF RICARDO'S PRESTIGIOUS RESTAURANT...

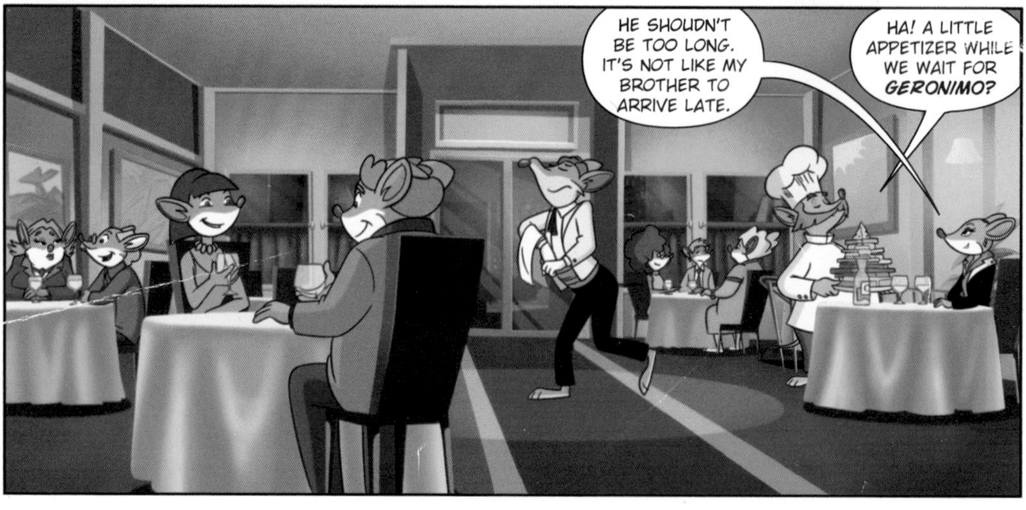
HA! A LITTLE APPETIZER WHILE WE WAIT FOR GERONIMO?
HE SHOUDN'T BE TOO LONG. IT'S NOT LIKE MY BROTHER TO ARRIVE LATE.

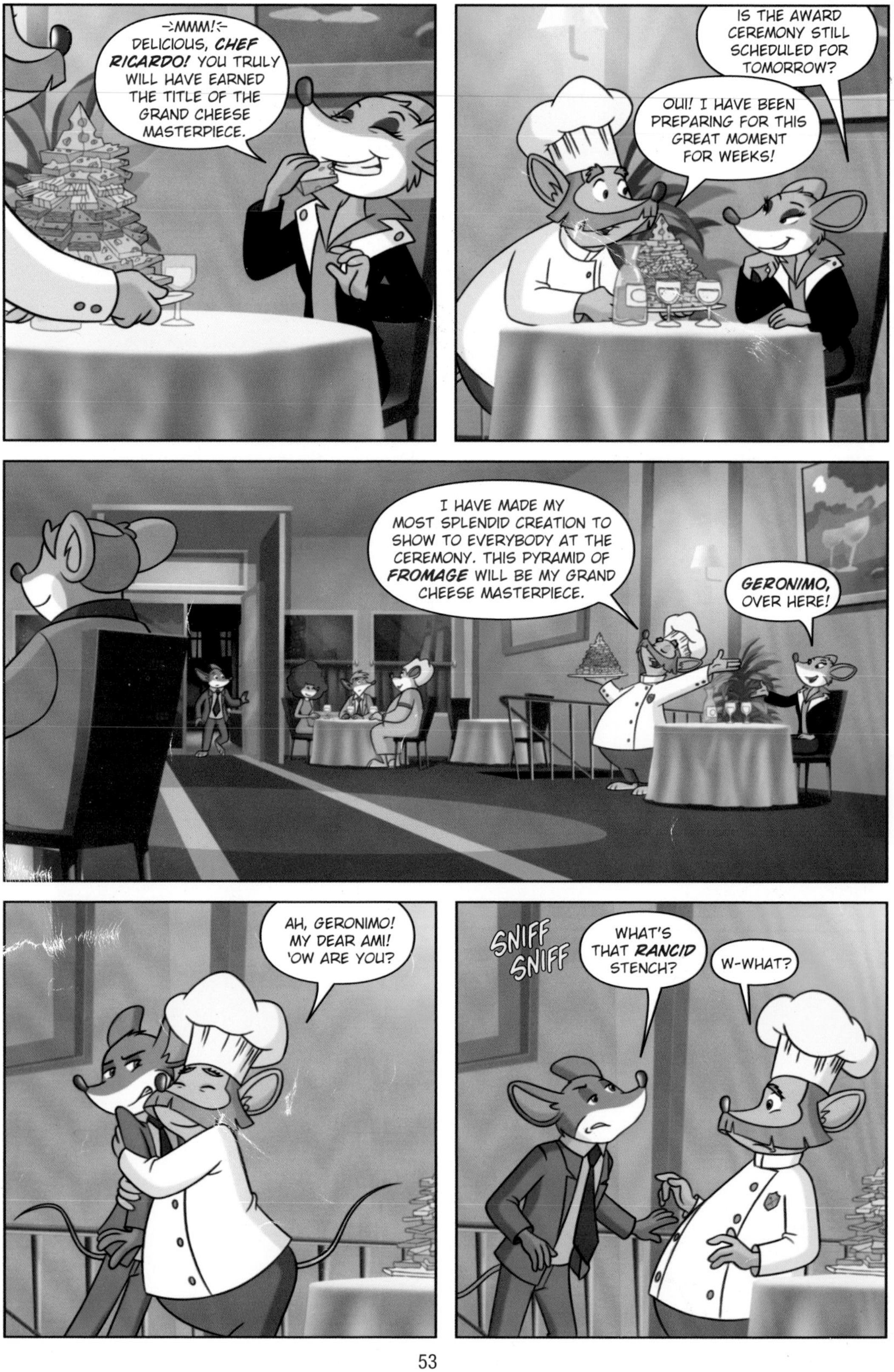
-MMM!-
DELICIOUS, CHEF RICARDO! YOU TRULY WILL HAVE EARNED THE TITLE OF THE GRAND CHEESE MASTERPIECE.
IS THE AWARD CEREMONY STILL SCHEDULED FOR TOMORROW?
OUI! I HAVE BEEN PREPARING FOR THIS GREAT MOMENT FOR WEEKS!
I HAVE MADE MY MOST SPLENDID CREATION TO SHOW TO EVERYBODY AT THE CEREMONY. THIS PYRAMID OF FROMAGE WILL BE MY GRAND CHEESE MASTERPIECE.
GERONIMO, OVER HERE!
AH, GERONIMO! MY DEAR AMI! 'OW ARE YOU?
SNIFF SNIFF
WHAT'S THAT RANCID STENCH?
W-WHAT?

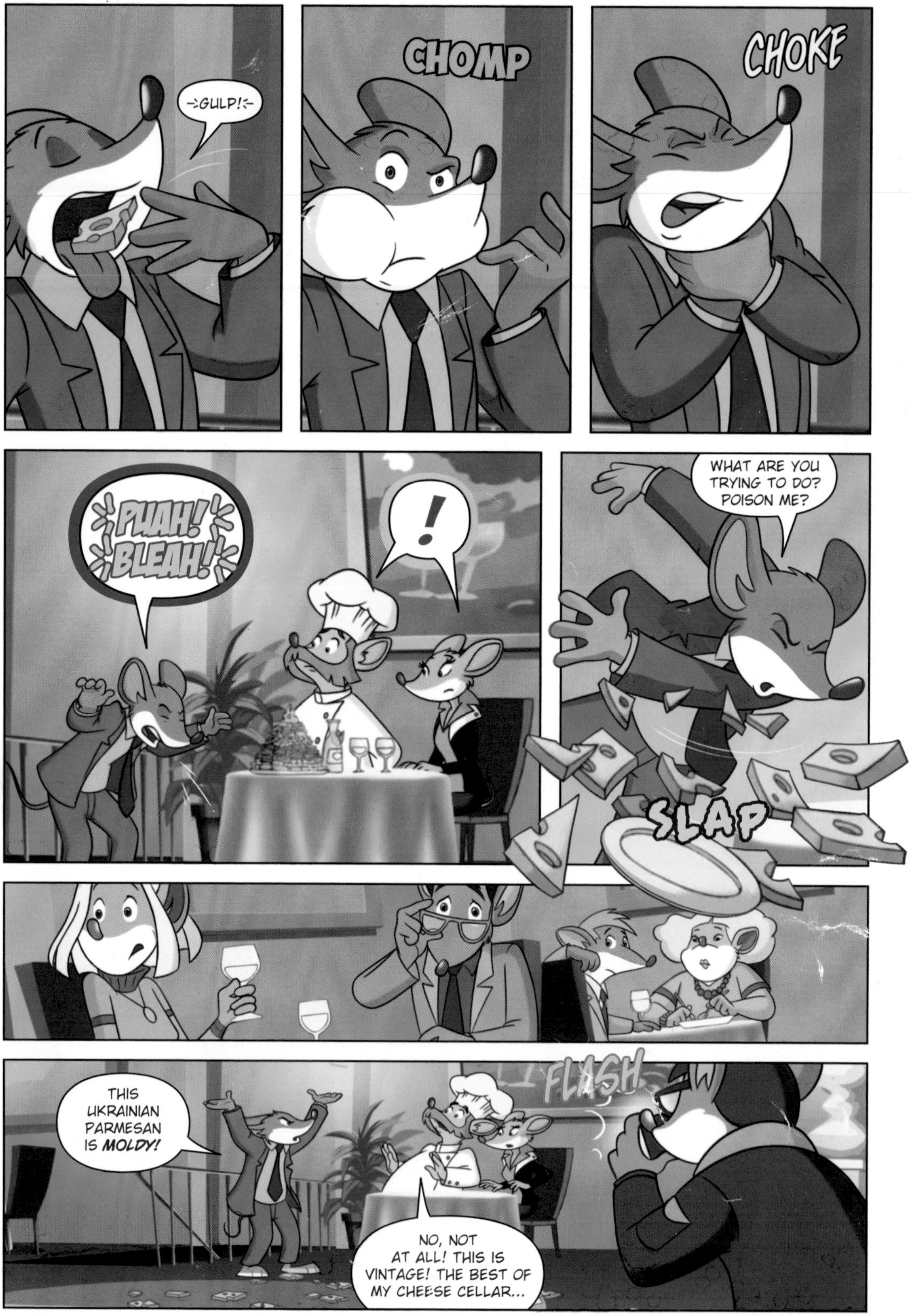
GULP!
CHOMP
CHOKE
PUAH! BLEAH!
!
WHAT ARE YOU TRYING TO DO? POISON ME?
SLAP
THIS UKRAINIAN PARMESAN IS *MOLDY!*
FLASH
NO, NOT AT ALL! THIS IS VINTAGE! THE BEST OF MY CHEESE CELLAR...

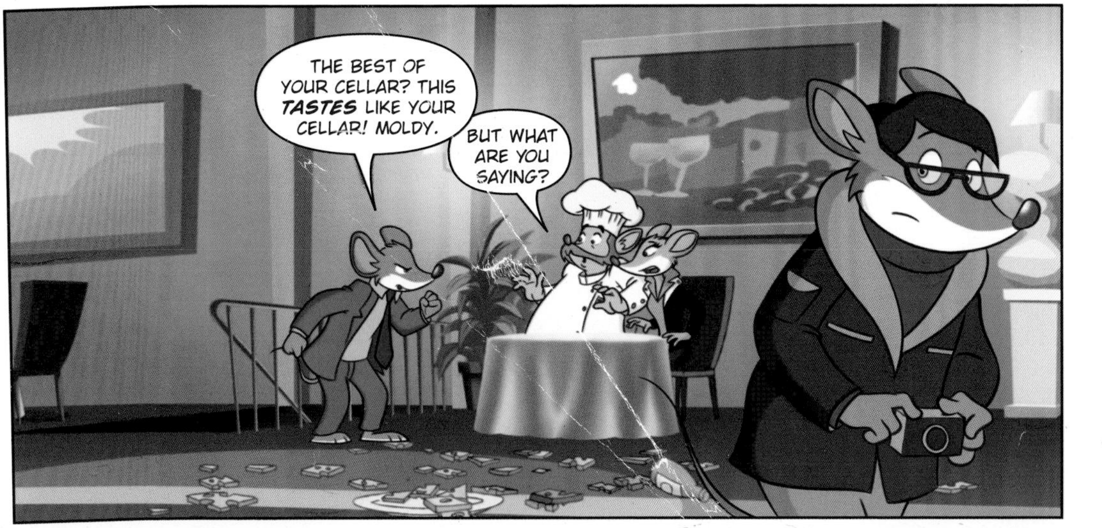
THE BEST OF YOUR CELLAR? THIS TASTES LIKE YOUR CELLAR! MOLDY.
BUT WHAT ARE YOU SAYING?

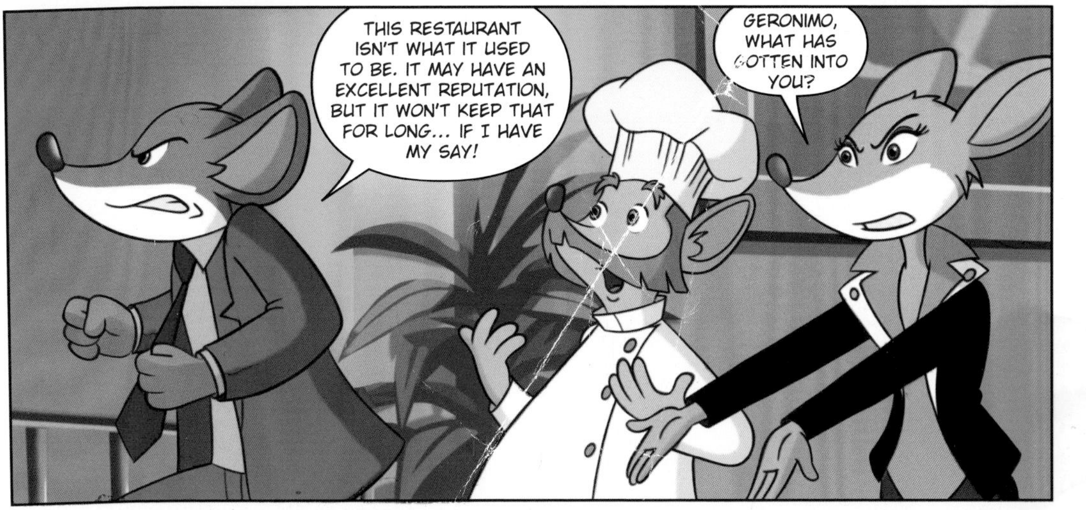
THIS RESTAURANT ISN'T WHAT IT USED TO BE. IT MAY HAVE AN EXCELLENT REPUTATION, BUT IT WON'T KEEP THAT FOR LONG... IF I HAVE MY SAY!
GERONIMO, WHAT HAS GOTTEN INTO YOU?

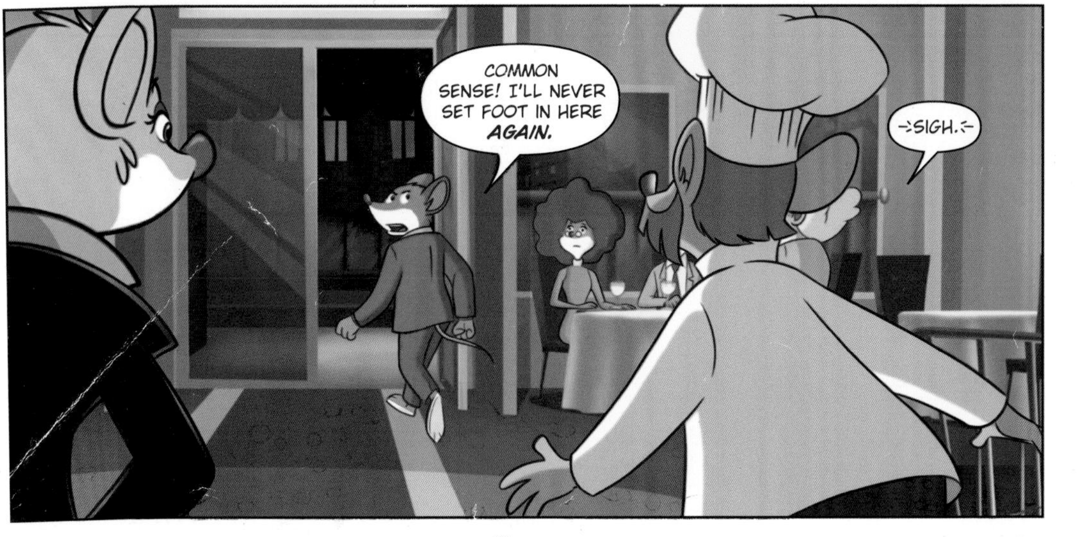
COMMON SENSE! I'LL NEVER SET FOOT IN HERE AGAIN.
SIGH.

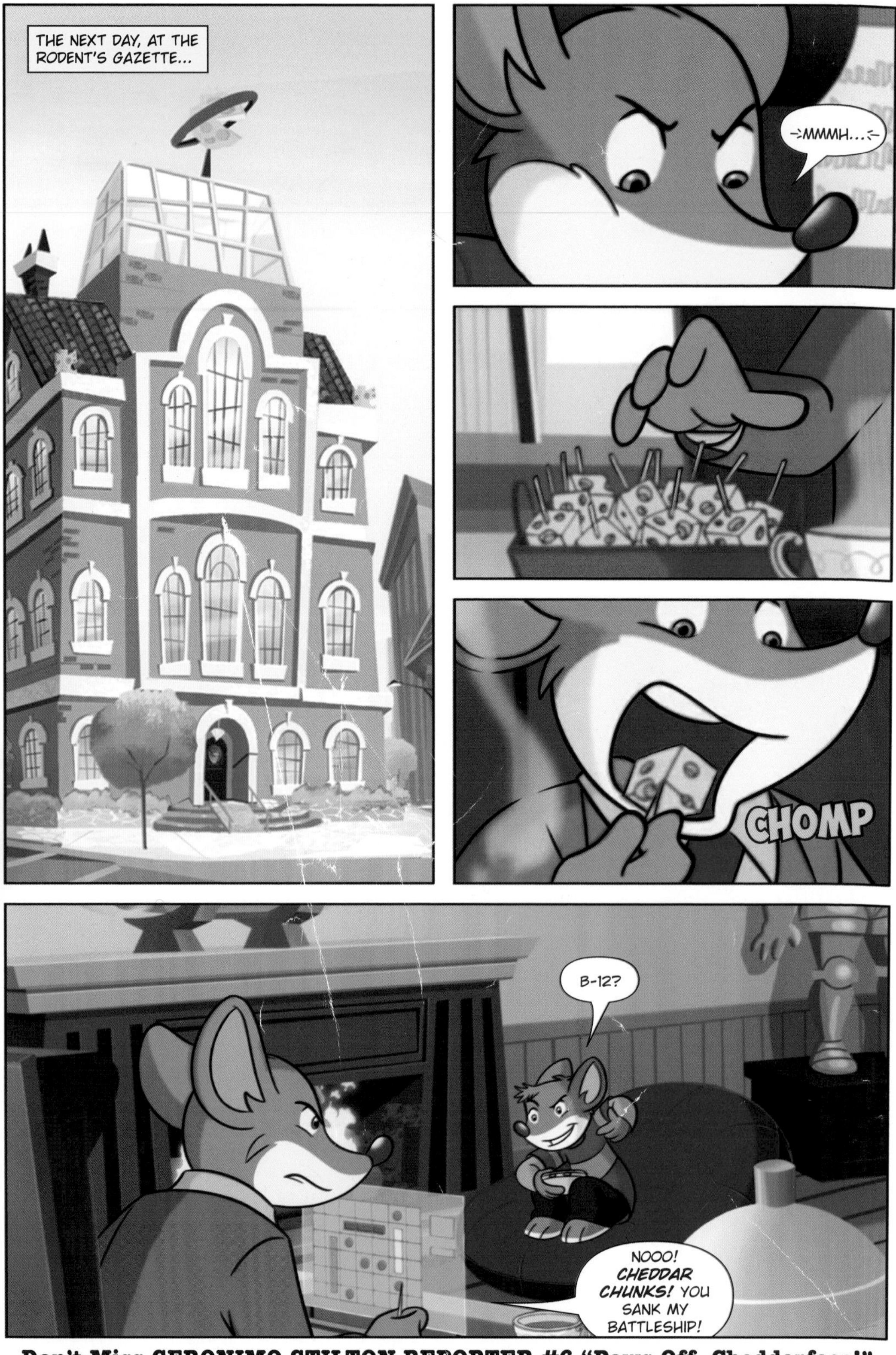
THE NEXT DAY, AT THE RODENT'S GAZETTE...
MMMH...
CHOMP
B-12?
NOOO! CHEDDAR CHUNKS! YOU SANK MY BATTLESHIP!

Don't Miss GERONIMO STILTON REPORTER #6 "Paws Off, Cheddarface!" Coming soon!

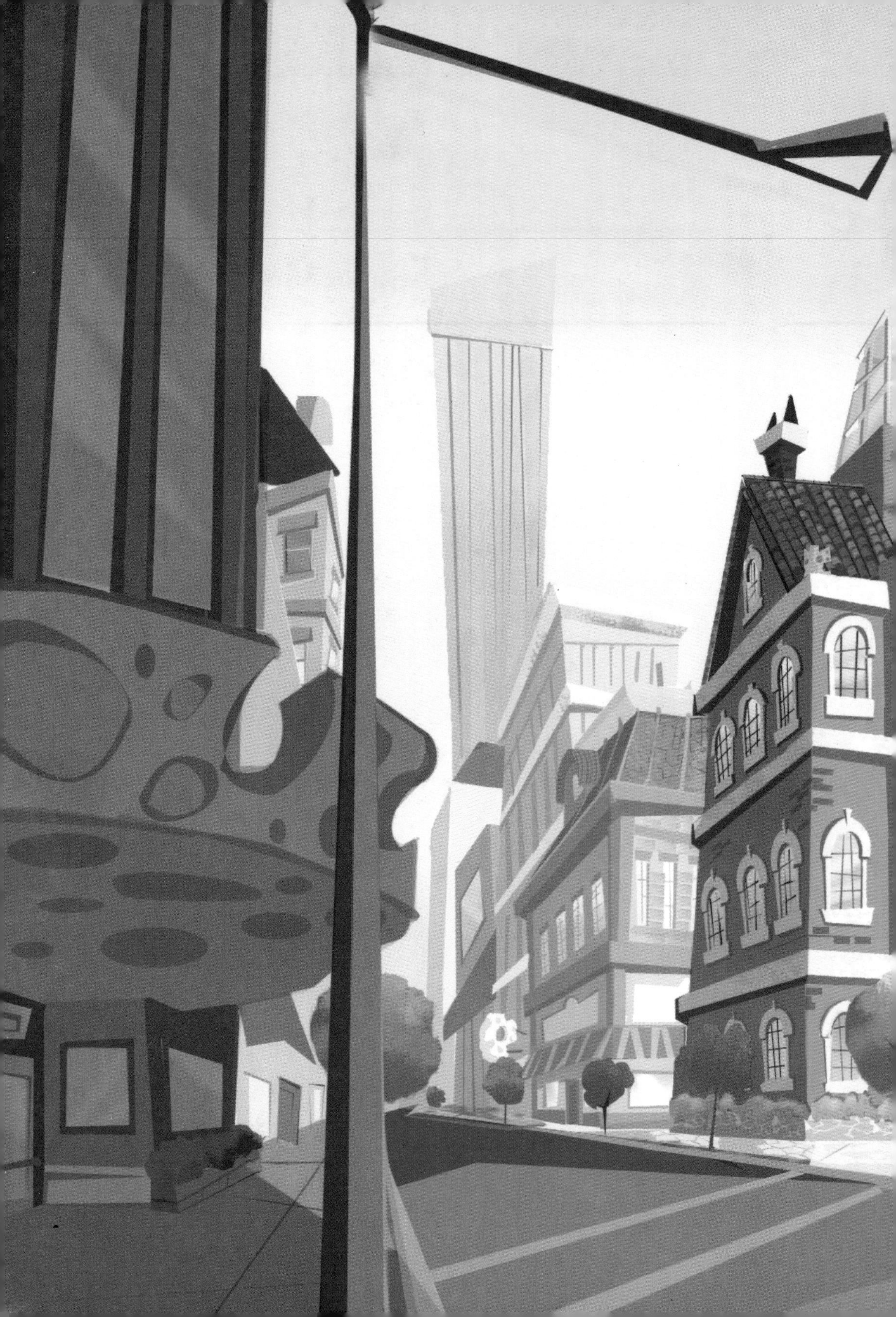